"This house is filled with my grandparents' spirits, Kelly."

Dalton's voice was a soft whisper. "I feel them in the middle of the night, hear them in the creaks and groans of the house. The overwhelming passion they felt for each other is all around us. Can't you feel it?"

He stood so close to her that his lips were mere inches from hers and the heat from his body seared through her.

Kelly hesitated, wanting to protest, to fight against the falling sensation, against the hypnotic power of his very presence. But she felt the ageless passions engulfing her, overwhelming her, and she knew Dalton was here to follow through on the restless energy, the intense desire, that pulsated between them.

"Yes," she whispered, and with that single acknowledgment, she knew she was lost....

Dear Reader,

Welcome back to the dark side of love. As we wind up our first year of publication, we're proud to bring you one author whose first Shadows novel appeared in our very first month and equally proud to offer you the first of what we hope will be many spooky tales by an author team new to the line.

Carla Cassidy's *Silent Screams* is just as scary as you'd expect it to be, coming from the author of *Swamp Secrets* and *Heart of the Beast*. It's a story of ghostly possession, and it takes place in an old mansion whose walls—if only they could talk—could tell tales of murder and betrayal and love everlasting. You, too, may scream—and not silently!—as you turn the pages.

Next up is *The Prince of Air and Darkness*, by two authors who write as Jeanne Rose. This is a wonderful blend of reality and myth and irresistible romance, a heady concoction that will stay with you long after you've finished the last chapter and set the book aside. And isn't that what haunting's really all about?

In months to come, as we start on Year Two, we'll be back with more of the wonderful mix of passion and peril that has come to mean reading pleasure to book lovers everywhere, the wonderful mix that is Silhouette Shadows. Until then—enjoy!

Leslie Wainger
Senior Editor and Editorial Coordinator

Please address questions and book requests to:
Reader Service
U.S.: P.O. Box 1325, Buffalo, NY 14269
Canadian: P.O. Box 1050, Niagara Falls, Ont. L2E 7G7

CARLA CASSIDY

SILENT SCREAMS

Published by Silhouette Books
America's Publisher of Contemporary Romance

SILHOUETTE BOOKS

ISBN 0-373-27025-9

SILENT SCREAMS

Copyright © 1994 by Carla Bracale

This edition published by arrangement with Harlequin Enterprises B. V.

® and TM are trademarks of Harlequin Enterprises B. V., used under license. Trademarks indicated with ® are registered in the United States Patent and Trademark Office, the Canadian Trade Marks Office and in other countries.

Printed in U.S.A.

Books by Carla Cassidy

Silhouette Shadows

Swamp Secrets #4
Heart of the Beast #11
Silent Screams #25

Silhouette Romance

Patchwork Family #818
Whatever Alex Wants... #856
Fire and Spice #884
Homespun Hearts #905
Golden Girl #924
Something New #942
Pixie Dust #958
The Littlest Matchmaker #978

Silhouette Desire

A Fleeting Moment #784

Silhouette Intimate Moments

One of the Good Guys #531

Silhouette Books

Silhouette Shadows '93
"Devil and the Deep Blue Sea"

CARLA CASSIDY

is the author of ten young-adult novels, as well as her many contemporary romances. She's been a cheerleader for the Kansas City Chiefs football team and has traveled the East Coast as a singer and dancer in a band, but the greatest pleasure she's had is in creating romance and happiness for readers.

This book is dedicated to Wendy Corsi Staub,
for her encouragement and support,
and Zasu Pitts,
for the haunting

CHAPTER ONE

Kelly Reynolds looked across the beach that separated the house from the ocean, noting the pieces of driftwood that dotted the sand, looking like half-finished bits of sculpture left unattended by a troubled artist.

The ocean crashed and thundered as it rolled to the sandy shore, the wildness of the water somehow matching the wildness of the house that sat nearby.

The house, rising out of the area of isolated Long Island beachfront, was a monstrosity. Constructed of wood and stone weathered to the color of the surrounding dunes, it was imposing, an architectural nightmare.

Boasting no particular style, the mansion contained hidden rooms and stairways to nowhere, all attesting to the madness that had eventually consumed the original owner.

"And it's all mine," she breathed to herself, still finding that fact difficult to believe. She settled back against the hard stone of the cement bench, her gaze captured by the house.

There were times when she wondered if she hadn't been just a little bit crazy herself in her intense desire to own the place. Its checkered past had daunted many a buyer.

Originally built by Randolf Weathers, a famous silent-film star, it had been occupied by Randolf and his wife, Daphne, for a little over a year. They had been a golden couple...until Randolf had plunged into a madness that had eventually resulted in their tragic deaths.

When Kelly first bought the house and had it renovated, she'd worried that the ancient tragedy might make the five individual apartments difficult to rent. But that hadn't been the case. First Jeffrey Richardson, a young art student, had contacted her about renting. Then Susan and Gary Philips, her best friends and avid old-movie buffs, had agreed to move in. Finally, Dalton Waverly, Randolf and Daphne's grandson, had called her to rent an apartment.

She leaned her head back and tilted it toward the early evening sun. The warmth was pleasing, but the air was unpleasantly thick and heavy, portending an approaching storm in the distance. She closed her eyes and thought about Dalton Waverly.

She had yet to meet him, although they'd had several phone conversations. He was working on a book about his infamous ancestor and had rented one of her apartments for six months, telling her he thought the ambience of the house would inspire him.

On an intellectual level she was anxious to actually meet him and learn more about the book he was writing about Randolf. But on an emotional level, something about Dalton Waverly's voice had unsettled her.

Although deeply masculine and attractive, she'd sensed a tension, a vibrant force coming from him, that had both intrigued and repelled her.

As a cloud moved over the sun, momentarily usurping the bright sunshine, she opened her eyes, her gaze automatically seeking the house once again.

It was a place that loved the shadows, seeming to grow and maintain an eerie nobility of its own in the dark shades of approaching night. And it was a house never completely silent. It whispered to itself in creaks and groans, as if loving the sound of its own voice.

In truth, the first couple of nights here alone, she'd been uneasy, unsettled by strange sensations. She'd felt as if the walls watched . . . waited . . . anticipating something Kelly was unaware of.

She knew some people would think she was crazy to imbue the wood-and-stone house with any human characteristics, but she'd always possessed a special sensitivity to space and energy, and this house positively throbbed with unseen energies.

It was the same with people. It was as if Kelly had a special insight into others' souls, and she was rarely wrong. There were times when she wasn't sure if the unique ability was a curse or a gift.

Again her thoughts drifted back to Dalton Waverly. She looked up at the small, round window in the third floor. She'd put Dalton in the attic rooms, anticipating that his poetic soul might enjoy the charm of the slanting eaves and rich woodwork. Besides, he'd mentioned that he intended spending a lot of time watching old reels of Randolf's movies. The attic dormer was long and narrow. It would make a perfect screening room.

She frowned slightly. There was something about the upstairs rooms that set her teeth on edge, filled her with anxiety. An energy there that gave her a feeling of not quite being alone. Although the unease she'd experienced in the rest of the house had somewhat dissipated, her disquiet regarding the attic had only intensified.

Initially, she'd worried about the rooms being too warm, worried that the air conditioner wouldn't be sufficient to cool the stale air. But she needn't have worried. Every time she'd been in the rooms she'd noticed a distinct chill. Apparently the insulation in the old house was better than she'd imagined.

She looked at her watch and smiled in anticipation. Not only was Jeffrey Richardson due to arrive anytime, but Susan and Gary as well. It would be wonderful to have people in the house once again. She'd go put on a pot of coffee.

Standing up, she stretched. Something at the attic window suddenly captured her attention. A flash of movement, then a glimpse of a pale form framed in stark relief.

She jumped and stifled a gasp, but when she looked again, the figure was gone and the window was just a round yawn of darkness.

Probably just a reflection of the sunlight, she thought uneasily, looking back to where the large dark cloud had moved away from the sun.

The unblocked sunlight painted the house in lush, golden tones, but didn't quite dispel the deep shadows that lingered around its edges. Once again, she looked up at the window, deciding that whatever she'd thought she'd seen was indeed nothing more than a trick of the sunlight playing peek-a-boo with the clouds.

And by the look of the dark clouds gathering on the horizon, there would definitely be a storm before nightfall. She would be interested in seeing how the roof fared in a heavy rain.

Checking her watch one last time, she went back into the house, anxious for her friends to arrive. The house needed people, needed laughter and life to chase away the pervasive gloom that seemed to wrap itself in and around her new home.

Once inside, she finished making the coffee, then sat down at the long wooden kitchen table to drink a cup of the brew. She sipped from her mug and gazed around her in satisfaction.

Yes, the workmen had done a good job, and she was particularly pleased that she'd been so cautious in choosing the furnishings for the house.

Some of the original furniture had been here when she'd bought it, and she'd used every piece, wanting to restore the house to the splendor it had once enjoyed.

She'd chosen the other furniture carefully, haunting antique stores and flea markets. She still had three rooms to decorate and had spent hours in the public library pouring over books and magazines, looking for pictures of how the rooms had actually looked when the famous couple had resided here.

She jumped, startled, as she heard a knock on the front door, but a smile of anticipation lifted her lips. Finally. Finally the house would live once again. Her footsteps rang hollowly as she crossed the empty living room and stepped into the marble-floored entry hall.

Opening the door eagerly, she greeted Jeffrey Richardson. He was a tall, thin young man with shoulder-length strawberry-blond hair and pale blue eyes. He smiled shyly, self-consciously tugging at the gold hoop decorating his ear. "All set for me to move in today?"

"All set," Kelly confirmed, noting the vast number of boxes he'd stacked on the front porch. "Need some help with those?"

"No thanks, I've got everything organized and I'd rather move them myself."

"Okay, you know the way. Just let me know if you need anything." She stepped aside as he picked up a box. She'd put Jeffrey in one of the two ground-floor apartments, assuming he'd probably be in and out of the house more frequently than the others.

As Jeffrey carried in box after box, Kelly returned to her coffee in the kitchen. She hoped the house would be happy with people once again occupying it. Besides the five individual apartments, there was also a large living room, library and kitchen that would serve as common rooms, available for use by everyone.

She smiled as she heard a stereo playing. Yes, it would be good to have the house filled with music and laughter... the sounds of people. Hopefully the life would banish the shadows she sensed in the hallways, erase the haunting remains of the tragic past and fill all the spaces with new, happy memories.

There was a rapid knock on the front door, and she hurried to answer it, knowing it was probably Susan and Gary. She opened the door and this time was instantly engulfed in a bear hug of mammoth proportions.

"Kelly!" Susan squealed, stepping back and looking at her, giving her friend's hands a tight squeeze. "Oh, hon, it's so good to see you."

"It's good to see both of you, too," Kelly said, reaching up to give the tall, solemn man next to Susan a kiss on his cheek. "Hi, Gary."

"Hi, Kell," he greeted her, breaking into a friendly, easy smile.

"Well, come on in," Kelly exclaimed, opening the door wider to allow them inside.

"Why don't I start carrying in boxes and stuff from the van," Gary said, shooting a fond grin at his wife. "I figure Susan's got another ten or fifteen minutes of squeals left in her and I don't think I can take any more."

"Oh, don't mind him. He's just testy because I made him buy me dinner on the way here," Susan replied, squealing yet again as Kelly led her into the house. "Look at this floor—it's magnificent."

"The architects tried to talk me into replacing it because it's cracked in several places, but I insisted we keep it."

"Just think, Randolf Weathers actually walked across this very floor." Susan sighed. "He was such a total hunk . . . too bad he was also totally nuts."

"His grandson, Dalton Waverly, should be arriving first thing in the morning. He's writing a book about Randolf and will be staying here for the next couple of months."

Susan frowned. "Another book on Randolf? There's been several written over the years."

Kelly shrugged. "I guess there will soon be another one."

Susan grinned at Kelly and linked arms with her. "Come on, show me this mansion of yours and where Gary and I are going to be living."

For the next few minutes Kelly showed Susan around the house, introducing her to Jeffrey, then leading her up the stairs to the second-floor apartment that would be the couple's home.

"It's just like you described it," Susan said as Kelly ushered her into the spacious studio apartment. "Oh, I'm so glad we decided to get out of the city and come here."

Kelly walked over to the window and drew back the heavy draperies. "You've got a beautiful view of the ocean from here." She frowned at the clouds, which had thickened considerably in the past few minutes. Black and roiling, they exuded a menacing energy, lightning flashing amid their dark depths. "We'd better help Gary get your things in. It looks like it's really going to storm."

It took them nearly an hour to unload the van. They were just carrying in the last of the boxes when the first raindrops splattered down to earth and thunder rumbled an ominous warning.

Laughing and shaking the droplets from her blond hair, Kelly ushered them into the kitchen for coffee. "Make yourself at home," she instructed, gesturing to the table. "Even though all the individual apartments have kitchenettes, I insisted they keep this original kitchen intact."

"This whole place is magnificent," Gary marveled, running a hand across the Italian tile countertop. "Just imagine if these walls could talk, what stories they could tell."

"I'm not sure I'd *want* to hear all the stories," Susan said as Kelly turned on the light to cut through the premature darkness brought on by the storm.

They all jumped as lightning crackled and thunder boomed. Kelly poured them coffee and joined them at the table, grinning at Susan, who she knew hated thunderstorms. "As strong as it's blowing out there, it will probably pass quickly," she said sympathetically.

"Good," Susan exclaimed, wincing as another flash of lightning momentarily illuminated the room and the light overhead blinked erratically. Susan shivered and took a sip of her coffee. "You know, I read one of those books about Randolf Weathers. Didn't he and his wife die right here in the house?"

Kelly nodded. "He pushed his wife down the stairs and shot her, then shot himself."

"How horrible." Susan took another drink from her cup, then wrapped her arms around herself, shivering yet again. "He must have been a dreadful man . . . completely insane."

"From what I've read, he was an alcoholic. Supposedly his career had hit the skids and he had horrible rages." Kelly paused a moment, then continued thoughtfully. "He was a brilliant man, but he must have had a tortured soul. Sometimes I think I can feel his and Daphne's spirit still lingering here in the house."

"Oh, come on, Kelly, stop it," Susan protested, her eyes widened in horror. "You know I hate it when you say stuff like that." Susan glared at her, then turned to Gary. "One night, when we were in college, a bunch of us messed around with a Ouija board and Kelly had me so thoroughly spooked I thought I'd never get to sleep."

Kelly laughed. "You spook easily." She turned and grinned at Gary. "She refused to keep the board in our room. She made me move it out into the hallway each night."

"It was scary. Kelly put her fingers on that pointer and it zoomed all over the letters, spelling all kinds of words and making weird sentences." Susan's words ended on a squeal as the lights overhead flickered twice, then remained off, plunging the kitchen into darkness.

"Take it easy, Susan. It's the storm, not anything supernatural," Kelly exclaimed. "You two just sit tight and I'll get some candles." Getting up, she rummaged in one of the cabinets, exclaiming in triumph as she withdrew two squat, fat candles. Lighting both, she placed one in the middle of the table and pocketed the matchbook, carefully balancing the other candle. "I'd better go check on Jeffrey and see that he has some sort of light or candles."

Holding the tiny flickering light before her, Kelly left Susan and Gary and entered the empty living room, where the little flame caused shadows to dance and sway on the walls like lost souls trapped within the Sheetrock.

As she reached the landing at the foot of the staircase, a shaft of cold air seemed to rise out of nowhere and engulf her. It extinguished the candle and raised goose bumps on Kelly's arms. Cold air swirled around her as if with a life of its own, curling first around her head and torso, then down the length of her legs.

For a long moment she stood completely still, swallowed by the arctic air and the surrounding darkness. Her heart pounded so loudly she could hear it echoing in her ears, and an inexplicable terror suffused her.

Then, as quickly as the cold had appeared, it disappeared, lifting away from her with the same sensation as that of a chill being shivered away.

Hands shaking, she withdrew the matches from her pocket and fumbled to light the candle once again, muttering a small protest as it took her three matches to finally get it lighted. A small measure of relief immediately swept through her at the radiant glow.

As she walked the rest of the way across the landing, she glanced up the wide, sweeping staircase and smiled in further relief. The window at the top of the landing was open. Although open only an inch or two, it was enough to allow in the cold storm winds.

She hurried up the stairs and closed it, feeling better, certain that it had been the cause for the strange cold air that had gripped her.

She went back downstairs and checked on Jeffrey, who she discovered had his own collection of scented candles, then returned to Susan and Gary.

"So, tell me about this Jeffrey," Susan said as Kelly poured them the last of the coffee.

Kelly smiled. "There isn't much to tell. He came out to look at the room two weeks ago, fell in love with the access to the beach. He's an artist, and according to what he told me, his parents are supporting him for the next year while he 'finds' himself."

"And what happens if he doesn't find himself in the next year?" Gary asked.

Kelly laughed. "Who knows? Then I suppose he'll have to put away his paintbrushes and get a regular job."

"Does he know about the history of this house?" Susan asked, shivering as thunder crashed and lightning rent the semidarkness of the room.

Kelly nodded. "I didn't think it was fair to ask anyone to live here without knowing the history and the tragedy of the place first."

"I almost wish *I* didn't know about it," Susan retorted. "Insanity and murder... I must be out of my mind to be staying here at all."

Gary laughed and took his wife's hand in his. "The past can't hurt you, my love. And I promise to protect you from all the things that might go bump in the night." He raised Susan's hand to his lips and kissed it. "Besides," he continued, "I don't believe in ghosts and goblins."

"Ah, my logical mathematician husband," Susan replied.

"Speaking of math..." Gary looked at his wristwatch. "I do have to go to work in the morning, and it's getting quite late."

Susan groaned and stood up. "And I've probably got a week's worth of unpacking ahead of me, starting in the morning."

"Kelly, we'll see you tomorrow," Gary said, taking their coffee cups and placing them in the sink.

Susan gave Kelly an affectionate hug. "I'm so glad we're here."

"Me, too. Here, you'd better take this." Kelly handed her the candle from the center of the table. "You'll need it to find your way."

"What about you?" Susan asked, taking the candle from her.

Kelly reached into the cabinet and withdrew another one and lit it off Susan's. "There. I'm all set. Hopefully the electricity will be back on by morning."

As Susan and Gary left to go to their upstairs apartment, Kelly carried the candle over to the sink. Rain lightly pattered against the windows and the sky outside still radiated with flashes of energy.

The house fell silent around her. It was an oppressive kind of silence, like that of the calm before the storm. She shoved the vague sense of unease away, realizing it was probably just tiredness. All the talk of Randolf and Daphne's deaths, coupled with the storm outside, had set her nerves slightly on edge.

Turning, she retrieved her coffee mug from the table and carried it to the sink, filling the sink with soapy water. The candlelight next to her created an eerie reflection on the glass of the window above the sink.

As she picked up the last mug to dry, lightning suddenly slashed the sky, illuminating a face that was staring into the window. A scream leapt to her lips and the mug crashed to the floor. In horror, she backed away from the window, her mind reeling in shock. Outside, black hair plastered slickly to his forehead, dark eyes glittering wildly, stood Randolf Weathers.

CHAPTER TWO

Kelly continued backing away from the window, the shards of the broken coffee mug crunching beneath her feet as she stared at the apparition at the window.

Another scream tangled up inside, trapped someplace between her chest and her throat. As she opened her mouth to release it, the ghost of Randolf Weathers tapped on the window.

"Hello? Miss Reynolds, is that you?"

She could hear the man's voice above the rumbling of the passing storm, and the scream trapped inside her instantly died away. She'd never had a ghost speak to her before, let alone call her Miss Reynolds. She took a step toward the window, wondering if she'd lost her mind.

"It's me...Dalton Waverly."

Kelly gasped. Dalton Waverly? He wasn't supposed to arrive until the next morning. What was he doing standing outside her kitchen window in the middle of a storm?

She ran to the back door and unlocked it, stepping aside to allow him entry. He swept in on a rush of cold wind and it was as if the storm itself invaded her kitchen. The temperature dropped as his eyes sought hers, eyes as dark as the night, eyes as turbulent as the raging elements outside. In the flickering candlelight he looked menacing, like the ghost of his crazed ancestor. Unconsciously Kelly took a step backward, away from Dalton Waverly's overwhelming presence.

His black hair was rain-slicked, emphasizing the hollows of his cheeks and the sensual fullness of his lower lip. His was a face of remarkable strength tempered with a kind of soulful depth, the same physical qualities that had made his grandfather a film star and heartthrob.

"I know I wasn't expected until tomorrow morning, but I got packed more quickly than I anticipated and decided to come on out tonight. I knocked on the front door, but nobody answered. I decided to walk around the back and saw the candlelight in the window." He shrugged out of his drenched jacket.

"Has anyone ever told you that..."

"That I look just like Randolf?" He smiled, a tight gesture that did nothing to alleviate the intensity radiating from him.

Beneath the lightweight jacket, he wore a pair of dark slacks and a pale blue shirt opened at the collar to expose a thatch of dark chest hair. He was the most attractive man Kelly had ever seen...yet something about him caused a flicker of unease to dance in the pit of her stomach.

It was amazing, really, how much he resembled his grandfather. Other than the fact that Randolf had always worn a well-trimmed mustache and Dalton didn't, it was almost like looking at a mirror image.

Kelly blushed, realizing she had been shamelessly staring at him.

"I'm really sorry you got so wet," she said. She held out her hand to take his coat, a snap of static electricity sparking as their fingers touched. She jumped back, a nervous burst of laughter escaping her lips. "The air is full of energy tonight," she said, taking his jacket and hanging it over the back of a chair. "I really apologize. I guess with the sounds of the storm and all, we didn't hear you knocking at the front door."

He merely nodded, his dark eyes fathomless as he gazed at her silently.

"Would you like for me to help you carry in your things?" she asked, noticing he carried nothing with him.

He shook his head, his eyes so like those of his ancestor, large and liquid, but cryptic. "I'll wait until morning to unload. I don't want anything getting wet."

"Okay, then why don't I take you right on up to your apartment?" Glad to be moving, Kelly picked up the candle from the countertop. "Unfortunately the electricity went off several hours ago and hasn't come back on yet."

As they walked out of the kitchen and across the large expanse of the living room, the candle flame once again caused eerie shadows to gyrate on the beige walls. "I'm still in the decorating process," she said to explain the emptiness of the room.

"It's an unusual house," he observed, his deep, rich voice sending a chill of pleasure down her back.

"Designed by an unusual man, from everything I've read." She started up the wide, curving stairway. "When the carpenters were doing the renovations, they found a hidden passageway and a staircase that leads to nowhere." She paused, waiting for him to catch up to her.

He moved slowly up the stairs, his hand lingering on the wooden banister as if, through his fingertips, he could absorb memories of the distant past.

"What a place this must have been when Randolf and Daphne lived here," he said softly. He joined her at the top of the stairs, his dark eyes lingering on her face.

He stood so close, he seemed to be breathing the air meant for her, making it difficult for her to catch her breath. "According to the books I've read, it was a real showplace before Randolf lost touch with reality," she said breathlessly.

"Ah, you read the Mesker book."

She nodded, self-consciously taking a step back from him. "Two summers ago," she answered, thinking of Gregory Mesker's book, entitled *A Plunge Into Madness*. It had been advertised as the definitive biography of Randolf Weathers and had topped the nonfiction bestseller list for some sixteen weeks.

Dalton's face tightened with an inexplicable tension, giving it an almost haunted look in the pale glow of the candle. "That piece of trash is part of what prompted me to write my own book."

Kelly, unsure what to say, merely nodded and led him up the second staircase, a narrow, steep one that continued to the attic rooms.

"I hope you don't mind I put you up here, but you mentioned on the phone that you plan to screen a lot of Randolf's old movies, and these rooms seem most conducive to that sort of thing."

"I'm sure it will be fine," he assured her.

"I believe originally Randolf had a study up here." She opened the door and shivered as a burst of chill air swept over her, through her. It was as if a draft of arctic air had been trapped inside, just waiting for the door to be opened so it could escape the confines of the attic. "Perhaps I should turn up the heat," she murmured. But once inside the room, the temperature seemed comfortable enough.

"That's not necessary," he protested, stepping into the room behind her. Immediately the ceiling light overhead flickered erratically...on, off, on, off. It blinked one last time, then remained off.

"The electric service company must be working on getting the power back on," Kelly observed, setting the candle down on the nearby coffee table. "The kitchenette is there." She pointed to the apartment-size appliances against one wall. He nodded and she pointed to another doorway. "And the bathroom is through that door over there."

He tilted his head to one side, as if listening to a voice or a sound only he could hear.

"You'll find that the house talks," she said impulsively, then blushed as he looked at her curiously. "It groans and moans, creaks and whispers. I'm just now starting to get used to it."

He smiled, a small gesture that did nothing to alleviate the darkness of his eyes. "I think I'm going to like it here." There was something in his gaze that made her think he wasn't just talking about the acceptability of the room, but about something more personal. . . .

"Well, I'll just let you get settled in, then." She felt her cheeks flaming brightly and was grateful for the deep shadows of the room. "Please let me know if you need anything. I'm in the apartment on the west side of the second floor."

She backed toward the door, finding her gaze once again lingering on the depths of his dark eyes. "Good night, Dalton."

"Good night, Kelly."

She turned to make a quick escape, but found that the utter darkness, without the aid of the candlelight, made a fast exit impossible.

She moved cautiously, her fingers touching the wall for orientation as she made her way back down the stairs, her head filled with thoughts of her newest guest.

One thing was for certain—he possessed the same kind of sensual magnetism as had his famous grandfather. Randolf had had a quality that made women swoon in the movie aisles. That same quality had been passed to his grandson.

It would be interesting to have him here for the next six months. Interesting and stimulating. She smiled at her own thoughts, honest enough to admit that she was incredibly attracted to him. She'd felt an immediate snap of electricity course through her when she'd realized he wasn't a ghost, but a flesh-and-blood man. Yet it was an attraction tempered with something else . . . a strange bit of trepidation.

She frowned, thinking of the dark energy that seemed to emanate from him. He certainly fit the old stereotype of a brooding, long-suffering writer. It had been something in his eyes . . . a haunted look that unsettled her.

As she entered her own apartment, she realized the storm had finally passed. A pale ghostlike strand of moonlight shone through her window, giving her enough light to undress and get into bed.

Her apartment was set up almost identically to the other four. Basically no more than large studios with a kitchenette and adjoining bath, the rooms were large and airy with space for an intimate sitting area.

And three of the four apartments were now filled with people. An artist, a writer, a struggling actress and a math teacher . . . a nice blend of personalities.

A sigh of contentment escaped her lips. She tensed as the house groaned, a deep low shifting sound, then seemed to release its own whispered sigh of satisfaction.

Kelly checked on the blueberry muffins baking in the oven. Seeing the tops were golden brown, she grabbed a hot pad and removed them, grateful that when she'd awakened an hour earlier, the power was back on.

As she filled the muffin pans once more with rich batter, she hoped everyone in the house had slept better than she had. She'd tossed and turned, plagued by dark dreams that had swirled around in her head all night long.

She'd awakened before dawn, exhausted but unable to go back to sleep and also unable to recall what the dreams had been about.

Now, with the storm of the night before a distant memory, and the sun shining brilliantly through her windows, the bad dreams seemed far away. She jumped as a knock sounded at the door, then hurried to answer. Opening the door, she grinned as Susan shuffled in, her furry bedroom slippers dragging across the carpeting.

"Good morning." Kelly grinned at her friend, remembering that Susan had never done mornings very well.

"Morning," Susan replied, beelining for Kelly's small table and flopping down in a chair. "Gary just left for work and I knew you'd be up and have coffee already made. It seemed easier to come in here and have a cup than dig through our boxes and try to find our coffeemaker."

Kelly grinned and poured her a cup. "Did you sleep well?"

"Like a log," Susan said, sipping the coffee with an appreciative sigh.

"Here, have a muffin." Kelly placed a basket of warm muffins on the table, then poured herself a cup of coffee and joined Susan.

"Hmm, this must be your grandmother's recipe," Susan observed as she bit into one of the muffins.

Kelly nodded, warmed by thoughts of the woman who'd raised her. "I bake them about once a week. It always makes me feel close to her."

Susan smiled sympathetically. "I was so sorry to hear about her passing away last year."

"She'd been sick for a long time. She was ready to let go." A wistful smile curved Kelly's lips. "Still, there are times I really wish she was here to see this place. She was so instrumental in my being able to buy it." Kelly thought of the inheritance she'd received from her grandmother, money that had allowed her to make a healthy down payment on this house.

"She'd be proud of what you've done."

"Yes, she would," Kelly agreed. "And she'd be thrilled that Randolf's grandson is living here."

"That's right, he's supposed to arrive sometime today." Susan grabbed another muffin from the basket.

"He came last night."

Susan's eyebrows shot up. "And? What's he like?"

Gorgeous, Kelly started to say, then hesitated. Gorgeous didn't even begin to describe Dalton Waverly. It didn't speak of his intensity, his overwhelming masculinity, the dark, provocative shadows in his eyes. "He's very attractive," she finally said.

"Hmm, do I detect a bit of romantic interest?" Susan asked curiously.

Kelly laughed. "Interest, yes. Romance...I don't know." She paused a moment to sip her coffee, then continued. "You know I've always been interested in the Randolf and Daphne tragedy. My interest in Dalton is just a reflection of that." Even as she said the words, she wondered if they were true. She had a feeling that even if Dalton was in no way connected with Randolf and Daphne, she'd still be attracted to him.

"Anyway," she quickly added, "I'm sure he'll be very busy working on his book."

"I thought everything that could be written about the Weathers already had been," Susan observed.

"So did I," Kelly agreed. "But apparently Dalton thinks differently."

"Well, I guess I'd better get back," Susan said, reluctantly pulling herself up out of the chair. "I've got an audition this afternoon and if I don't find the coffeepot before I leave so Gary can make coffee when he gets home from work, he'll be one unhappy camper."

"What's the audition for?"

"A commercial for a fast-food chain." Susan rolled her eyes dramatically. "If I get it, it will probably involve dressing up like a hamburger or a piece of fried chicken."

Kelly laughed, trying to imagine her slender friend dressed up like a sandwich. "Who knows, you may gain world fame as the french-fry queen."

"Heaven forbid," Susan groaned. Then, giving a little wave, she left and went back to her own apartment.

Kelly remained at the table, relaxing with a cup of coffee, thinking of Susan and her aspirations of being an actress. There were times Kelly was amazed that she and Susan had clicked so nicely as friends. And in the five years since their graduation from college, they had maintained the friendship.

Susan had a flair for the flamboyant. She overacted dreadfully offstage, but showed promising talent onstage. She was an extrovert, while Kelly was often accused of being aloof because of her more introverted personality.

Her grandmother had always told Kelly that her reclusive tendencies were a form of self-protection, a way to distance herself from the acute sensitivity to others' emotions. And there were times when Kelly wondered if perhaps she'd subconsciously chosen her job of writing computer programs for that very reason—because it required very little interaction with other people.

She did love people, it was just the vibrations she sometimes picked up from them that often made her uncomfortable. Of course, Susan's didn't. Susan radiated a bright yellow energy, one of high spirits, optimism and cheerfulness. Gary's was a mint green, cool and calm. From what little time she'd spent around Jeffrey, it was difficult to pick up on the colors of his energies.

She finished baking the rest of the muffins, then spent the remainder of the morning at her computer, working on a bookkeeping program for a nearby doctor's office. At noon she stopped working, fixed herself a sandwich and went to the window that overlooked the beach. Jeffrey was there, an easel holding the canvas he was working on. She smiled at the picture he made. In his baggy slacks and oversize shirt, with his shoulder-length hair blowing in the wind, he looked every bit the bohemian artist at work.

Earlier she'd heard some activity on the stairs and had peeked out to see Dalton carrying up boxes. She assumed he was busy getting settled in.

She'd just finished her sandwich and was trying to decide whether to get back to the computer program or work on stripping the last of the old paper off the living room walls when there was a knock on her door. She opened it to Dalton.

"I'm sorry to bother you, but I was wondering if you could tell me where the nearest grocery store is. I brought everything I would need for the next six months except food."

"Sure, there's one in the next block." Kelly was unsurprised to see that he was just as handsome in the light of day as he'd been the night before in the shadows of the storm. Still, there was that dark intensity about him that was slightly unsettling.

"Also, when you get a chance, would it be possible for you to take me on a tour of the house? I'd love to see it all."

"I've got some time right now if you'd like," she suggested tentatively.

"That would be terrific." He smiled, but once again Kelly noticed the gesture didn't begin to reach the depths of his ebony eyes.

With a self-conscious smile of her own, Kelly closed her apartment door and led him down the stairs and into the huge, empty living room. "As I mentioned to you last night, I'm just getting started on the decorating of this room. I've got wallpaper ordered for in here."

"It's going to be quite a job," he observed, looking up at the high ceilings and the remaining stained wallpaper hanging off one wall.

"Yes, but it's a labor of love."

"How long have you lived here?" he asked, moving over to the window and staring outside.

"I've owned the house almost five months, but it's taken four of those months to get it ready for occupancy," she explained. "The basic structure was set up beautifully to accommodate five individual apartments. Two on both the first and second floor, then yours in the attic."

He nodded and followed her out of the living room and into the study. A stone fireplace took up one entire wall and bookshelves lined the others. A love seat and two wing chairs sat before the fireplace, inviting one to sit and stare into the fire or enjoy one of the many books on the shelves. A gleaming mahogany portable bar sat in one corner, displaying several decanters of liquors. A door led out to a small cement patio, and a concrete bench there looked out over the beach.

Dalton ran a hand across the carved back of the love seat. "This is nice," he observed.

"I wanted a sort of community room where any of my tenants could come and relax and enjoy each other's company." Kelly couldn't help the pride that crept into her voice. "I've tried to keep everything as close as possible to the way Randolf and Daphne had the house decorated. Some of the books on the shelves were found in a box down in the basement. Feel free to use any of them."

"Would you mind if I use this room this evening?" he asked suddenly. "I've got an older man coming for an interview and the stairs up to my place might be a bit much for him."

"Not at all. That's what this room is for."

He turned and looked at her, his expression inscrutable. "Since you seem to have an interest in Randolf and Daphne, you might want to join us here this evening. The man I'm interviewing is Malcolm Jennings."

"Malcolm Jennings... Wasn't he Randolf's agent?" Kelly asked.

"Agent and best friend," Dalton explained. "He heard I was working on a new book and called me several days ago to offer his assistance."

"Didn't he help write the Mesker biography on Randolf?"

Dalton's facial features tightened and his jaw clenched. "That's right, he did, but I've discovered a lot of inconsistencies in that piece of work that I want to straighten out.''

''Well, I don't know about sitting in on your interview, but I'd love to meet him.''

She took him into the kitchen, where he ran his hand over the Italian tile and stood for a long moment at the window that looked out on the beach. ''Who's the artist?'' he asked.

''That's Jeffrey. He lives in the apartment on this floor.'' Kelly smiled and looked out the window herself, seeing that Jeffrey had abandoned his easel and was now stretched out on the blanket with his shirt off. ''He's a very young nineteen years old and he's trying to find himself.''

Dalton turned and gazed at her, a dark eyebrow quirked upward. ''And he thinks he'll do that by tanning on the beach?''

Kelly laughed, slightly unnerved by the directness of his gaze. ''I said he was young.''

Together they left the window and the kitchen. ''The rest of this floor is taken up with Jeffrey's apartment and one that's presently unrented. Upstairs there's my apartment, and Susan and Gary Philips'—they're friends of mine,'' she explained. ''But there are also several interesting structural anomalies up there.''

She was acutely conscious of Dalton behind her as he followed her to the second floor of the house. But when she reached the landing, she realized he wasn't right behind her.

Turning around, she saw him lingering halfway up the staircase, his hand touching the wood of the banister, his head tilted to one side in the curious manner he'd shown the night before.

"Sorry," he said, suddenly realizing she was waiting for him. He moved up the remainder of the stairs slowly, his hand caressing the railing. "You can almost hear the past whispering its secrets here," he said softly. He stepped up beside her on the landing, standing so close she could smell the evocative scent of his cologne, feel the heat of his body and a strange vibrating energy coming from him.

She stepped back, not wanting to feel his vibrations, not wanting to pick up any sensation from him. She sensed a darkness there, a powerful darkness that magnetically pulled at her. "My friend Gary says that the past can't hurt us," she said with forced lightness.

"Then your friend Gary is a fool." Again the tension was back on his face. "The past is an ominous power that directs the present and predicts the future." His eyes grew distant, black pools of thought turned inward. "The death of my grandparents has haunted me and my family for years. Worse than their tragic deaths are the way they've been picked over by the authors of books of myth and rumor. Like carrions on corpses, these writers gnawed and chewed on the memory of my grandfather, portraying him as the embodiment of evil."

Kelly felt his energy swirling around her. Black and angry, it threatened to overwhelm her in its fury. But beneath the rage, she also felt frustration and a strange indefinable need.

He looked over the railing to the landing below and continued. "My grandfather's been depicted by writers as an alcoholic, power-hungry, insane man who willingly chose to kill his wife. But the personal letters and journals I've got show him to be a passionate, loving man who had his demons, but would never be capable of shoving the woman he loved down a flight of stairs, then taking a gun and shooting her in the head."

"So, what's the truth?" Kelly asked.

He glanced at her, his energy field waning as he frowned thoughtfully. "I don't know. That's what I'm here to find out."

"And how do you intend to do that?" she asked curiously.

"Research. I've got books and old journals, contracts and legal papers from my mother. She was only five years old when my grandparents died, and Mom kept boxes of things from the estate for years. She gave them to me six months ago, just before she passed away."

His eyes were once again dark, fathomless pits as he looked down at the landing beneath them...the landing where Daphne and Randolf had died so many years before. Reaching up, he raked a hand through his thick, dark hair. "I've just started going through all the paperwork to see if I can discover anything new about that night." He turned fully and pinned her with laserlike intensity, his eyes haunted and as black as raven wings. "I need to know the truth. I need to somehow crawl into Randolf's head."

Kelly felt a sudden, inexplicable shiver of apprehension shimmy up her spine at his intensity. She followed his gaze to the bottom of the staircase. She stared back at Dalton, wondering what ghosts he might stir up in his efforts to know intimately his brutal, mad ancestor.

CHAPTER THREE

Dalton leaned back in his chair and rubbed his forehead tiredly. For the past three hours he'd been immersed in research, digging through a file of old contracts that displayed the initial professional success of Randolf Weathers.

Shoving back from the paper-laden table, Dalton stood up, stretching his arms overhead to relieve the kinks that had taken up residency while he sat.

After Kelly had taken him on the tour of the house, he'd gone to the nearby grocery store and stocked the cabinets and refrigerator. His rumbling stomach now reminded him that he hadn't eaten all day and it was time for dinner.

Reaching into the freezer, he pulled out a TV dinner and popped it into the oven, not wanting the hassle of cooking something more elaborate. Turning on the oven to the required temperature, he then grabbed a cup of coffee from the pot warming on the stove. He took a sip and moved over to stand at the porthole window.

The view was phenomenal, allowing him to enjoy a vast expanse of beach and water. He knew if he cracked the window open he would be able to hear the ocean as it rolled to shore, smell the scent of sundried kelp and the salt-tinged breeze.

He touched his temple, wishing he'd remembered to buy aspirin when he'd stocked his small kitchen. He couldn't seem to shake the headache that had been a nagging irritant all morning.

As he sipped his coffee, his gaze drifted away from the water, to the stone bench directly below his room. Kelly was there. She sat with her head tipped back, as if enjoying the warmth of the sun's rays on her face.

He frowned, remembering the night before, when he'd first spied her through the kitchen window. He'd stood there in the rain for several minutes, merely watching her, before knocking to get her attention. The candlelight had danced in her pale gold hair and had given her an ethereal quality that for a moment had mesmerized him.

She was attractive, there was no doubt about it. Her straight blond hair and large green eyes were enhanced by her heart-shaped face and delicate features. Yes, she was definitely pretty, and he'd instantly felt a flash of attraction to her.

He turned away from the window with a sigh of frustration. He didn't have time for a romantic liaison, nor did he have the desire to pursue one. He had only one goal that burned in his heart . . . to vindicate his grandfather and remove the cloud that had hung over the family for too long.

Dalton had always felt a special affinity for Randolf, perhaps in part due to his amazing physical similarity to the man. But it hadn't been until the past year, when Dalton had turned the same age as Randolf at his death, that Dalton's interest in his grandparents had grown to the level of an obsession.

Since turning thirty-five, he'd developed a strange new kinship to his ancestor, a consuming need to delve into the past. It frightened him sometimes, the compulsive need he'd acquired to dig into a crime that had happened years before. It was like being stricken with a dread disease, and it was something he felt he wasn't in control of, as if a powerful force guided him, controlled him.

It had begun when his mother had been diagnosed with cancer, and realizing her time was limited, had begun to mentally resolve issues. But the one issue she couldn't resolve was her father's madness and the image of him portrayed by the gossipmongers. It was in direct contrast to her distant memories of her first five years of life. And yet...for years she'd suffered nightmares of one particular night. The crime that had taken place that night had marked her as emotionally as if she'd committed it herself. Psychologically, at least, she'd never really been able to move on, put it in the past where it belonged.

Before her death, Dalton had spent hours next to her bedside, listening to those memories, trying to weed out fact from fiction, reality from myth. The end result had been a blending of both, leaving the truth about the real character of Randolf still an elusive mystery, the circumstances surrounding his and Daphne's deaths a puzzle. But Dalton hoped that in discovering whatever facts there were behind the hor-

rendous murder/suicide, the truth would hold an ex-
oneration of blame for Randolf.

What if it doesn't? a small voice niggled in the back
of his head. What if you discover that the truth is that
Randolf was truly insane, an evil man who surrendered to the black forces of rage and jealousy?

Dalton rubbed his temple once again, his headache
pounding ferociously. That voice continued relent-
lessly. And what if you not only inherited his physical
traits, but his mental ones as well? That was a fear that
gnawed at him day and night. He knew how alike he
and his grandfather were.... How deep did the resemblance go?

He threw himself back down in the chair at the table, refusing to even contemplate the very possibility
that he might have inherited his grandfather's insanity.

Kelly hurried to answer the doorbell, looking at her
wristwatch as she walked. Seven o'clock. Dalton had
told her Malcolm Jennings would arrive around seven.
The old man was not only a legend, but apparently
punctual as well.

Kelly had seen many pictures of Malcolm Jennings, ancient pictures of him with his arm around a
movie star, signing contracts for another deal, on the
set of a movie. He'd been frozen in her mind as the
youthful, successful agent to the stars.

When she opened the door to greet him, she realized immediately how old those photos had been, but
she was pleased to see that the passing of time had

been kind to Malcolm. His silver hair was thick and luxurious, framing a face where deep wrinkles only added character. He was small for a man, several inches shorter than Kelly's own five foot seven, but there was a presence about him that made him appear taller.

She noticed the car in front of the house, a white limousine of impressive length. The man obviously traveled in style.

"My dear, I'm here to see Dalton Waverly." His voice was deep and smoothly cultured, reminding Kelly that this was a man who had once held the power to make and break careers, who had once been courted by some of the most influential men in the movie industry.

"Yes, of course, Mr. Jennings. I'm Kelly Reynolds. Please, come in."

He nodded and entered the hallway. He paused, merely standing for a moment and looking around, his blue eyes distant, as if seeing the area in another space and time.

"It's been so many years," he murmured more to himself than to Kelly. Then he smiled at her. "I lived here years ago, you know."

"No, I didn't know," Kelly answered in surprise.

He nodded. "When Randolf and Daphne first built the house, I moved in for almost a year." His eyes became reflective once again. "One of the happiest times of my life." He shook his head, as if mentally placing himself in the here and now. "I understand Dalton is the Weathers' grandson. I remember his mother quite well, a sweet, quiet child. I'm most anxious to meet him."

"And I'm sure he's looking forward to meeting you, too." Kelly gestured toward the study. "If you'll just have a seat and make yourself at home, I'll tell Dalton that you're here."

He inclined his head in a gracious nod as he sat down in one of the wing chairs. Kelly left him there and hurried up the stairs toward Dalton's room.

She met him coming out of his room, notebook and tape recorder in hand. "I was just coming to tell you Malcolm has arrived," she said.

"Good. I'm all ready for him." He moved past her and partway down the stairs, then turned back. "Aren't you joining us? I know how interested you are in Randolf and Daphne."

"I don't want to intrude," Kelly replied hesitantly, torn between her desire to listen to their conversation and not wanting to make a pest of herself.

"You won't be intruding," he assured her.

"Then I'd love to join you," she replied.

Together they descended the stairs and went into the study, where Malcolm stood with his back to the door, looking at the books on the shelves.

"Mr. Jennings?"

He turned at the sound of her voice, the pleasant expression on his face usurped by a look of horror when he saw Dalton. He stumbled backward, bumping hard into the bookcase behind him.

"Mr. Jennings, this is Dalton Waverly," Kelly hurriedly said, reaching out a hand to steady the old man. "Randolf's grandson."

"Grandson? Oh, of course." Malcolm eased himself back down into the wing chair with a small laugh. "My goodness, for a moment there I thought Randolf was standing in the doorway." He studied Dalton, his eyes narrowed a bit. "Actually, while there is an amazing physical resemblance, there are some strong dissimilarities as well. Randolf was slighter. He didn't have your breadth of shoulder. In fact, most of the time he wore jackets with padding to give him the appearance of broad shoulders."

"Indeed?" Dalton's black eyebrows raised as he took the high-backed chair across from Jennings. Forgotten for the moment, Kelly moved to the love seat quietly and sat down.

"Oh, Randolf was terribly self-conscious about it," Malcolm continued. "He worked out with weights, trying to build bigger shoulders, but it never did much good." He paused, then said, "I understand you're working on a book about your grandfather."

Dalton nodded, his dark eyes inscrutable.

"Why?" Malcolm asked. "There have been several written already."

"Biographies unauthorized by the family, written with an eye toward sensationalism," Dalton clipped out.

Kelly was suddenly aware of a vibrating tension in the air between the two men, a tension as palpable as the textured material of the love seat beneath her fingertips.

"Sensationalism..." Malcolm repeated the word with a touch of wry humor. "I'd say Randolf and Daphne's life-style lent itself to sensationalism." He smiled at them both. "You're aware that I coauthored the Mesker book."

"I'm aware," Dalton answered succinctly.

It was then Kelly realized what the energy was between the two men. It was the competitiveness of two authors sizing each other up. She knew that Dalton hadn't liked the Mesker portrayal of Randolf, and Dalton's dislike was obviously apparent to Malcolm.

"And you don't agree with the contents of that book?" Malcolm asked, his gray eyebrows rising on his forehead.

"I'm not sure what to think. I only know that the Mesker book was slanted toward satisfying a bloodthirsty public." Dalton's stare was long and hard on the old man. "And that this is a book I need to write. Since you spent so many years close to Randolf, I appreciate you offering to allow me to interview you."

Malcolm nodded. "When I read that you were beginning work on a book about Randolf, I knew I could probably be a valuable source. After all, I was closer to Randolf and Daphne than anyone."

Dalton set his tape recorder on the coffee table. "Do you mind if I use this?"

"Not at all," Malcolm said.

"Before you get started, would either of you like something to drink?" Kelly asked.

"Oh, I'd love a cup of hot tea, if that's possible," Malcolm said. "I generally have a cup or two in the evenings."

Kelly nodded and looked at Dalton. "Nothing for me," he said. She hurried from the room, hoping the two of them didn't say too much before she returned.

It took only minutes for her to prepare a tray and wait for the whistling shriek of the teakettle. Once the water was hot she poured it into the ceramic teapot, then hurried back into the study.

As she reentered the room, she heard Malcolm telling Dalton how he had first discovered Randolf in a small community theater in upstate New York. He didn't pause in his story as he poured his own tea and added sugar. Kelly sat herself down on the sofa, trying to focus on what he was saying.

However, she'd heard the story of Randolf's discovery before, read about it dozens of times in old movie magazines. Which was why, in spite of her interest, she found her concentration drifting, her gaze drawn again and again to Dalton.

He held the notepad in his lap, a pencil in his fingers, but he took no notes and instead was focused intently on Malcolm. Kelly found herself studying Dalton's hands. They were nice, long, artistic fingers with short, well-trimmed nails. Artistic, but possessing strength.... Capable hands.

There was something about him that was magnetic, electrifying, something that touched her profoundly. She sensed a simmering rage of sorts inside him, a force scarcely contained, a need barely suppressed.

From what she had seen, it had been that way with Randolf, too. On-screen, he'd been a simmering cauldron of emotions, and the audience's fascination had been, in part, an anticipation of the inevitable explosion.

"I'm afraid you won't like what you learn about your grandfather," Malcolm was saying, pulling Kelly's focus from her thoughts and back to the conversation at hand.

"I'm prepared for that," Dalton said, his dark eyes reflecting an inner torment. "Believe me, I've heard all the stories, read all the reports. I've heard he was an alcoholic, that he had a horrible temper and that he was obsessively jealous where my grandmother was concerned."

"It was more than that. At the end, Randolf was quite simply mad." Malcolm paused a moment and sipped his tea. He smiled at Kelly. "Thank you, my dear. This is quite good." He settled back in the seat and sighed. "It's hell getting old. There was a time when I didn't go to bed until I'd had a couple of snifters of brandy. Now a single shot puts me directly to sleep." He closed his eyes for a moment, then looked at Dalton. "Did you know I lived here with Randolf and Daphne for a while?"

"No, I didn't know that," Dalton answered with surprise.

"I stayed here with them for almost a year. I moved out three months before that last night—" He broke off, leaning his head back and staring at the ceiling. "There are times when I think that if I hadn't moved out—if I'd still been staying here—then the whole thing wouldn't have happened at all."

"There was a party that night, wasn't there?" Kelly asked, then flushed and looked apologetically at Dalton. He'd said she could sit in on the interview, but that didn't mean he wanted her to help conduct it. But he didn't seem to mind. He nodded at her, then looked at Malcolm expectantly.

"Oh, what a party it was." A smile touched Malcolm's lips. "An anniversary party, and the house was bedecked with balloons and streamers. Florists and caterers ran in and out of the house for two days before it, bringing in huge floral bouquets and checking and rechecking menus. Daphne never did anything halfway and there was nobody who loved a party more than she did."

"Tell me about her," Dalton prompted. "There is so much written and speculated about Randolf, but in comparison there's very little about Daphne."

Malcolm's eyes seemed to soften and his smile deepened. "Daphne was a true lady. Aside from her physical beauty, she had a beauty of spirit that made one feel special whenever in her company. Of course, I knew her when she was Daphne Windsor, a struggling actress awaiting her big break. I took her with me one evening to see Randolf performing at a small theater in New York City." His hands clenched into fists. "It was me who introduced the two of them and set the fates on their course of destiny." His smile faded and his lips quivered. "I rue the day I brought them together." His voice broke and he seemed to melt down into the chair, suddenly looking years older.

"Mr. Jennings, are you all right?" Kelly asked worriedly, seeing the paleness of the man's complexion.

"Yes my dear, I'm fine." He looked at Dalton. "I'm afraid we'll have to cut this interview short. I had a busy day and didn't realize how utterly exhausted I am."

"Of course," Dalton agreed, shutting off the tape recorder.

"Perhaps we could continue sometime tomorrow afternoon?" Malcolm suggested, rising out of his chair to a chorus of old bones popping and creaking.

Dalton also stood, setting his notebook on the coffee table. "Whenever is convenient for you. I'll be more than happy to work around your schedule."

Malcolm smiled, some of the color returning to his face. "At my age, the only schedule I keep is the one my body insists upon. Why don't I plan to be back here around two tomorrow afternoon? Early afternoon seems to be my peak time."

Dalton nodded his agreement and together he and Kelly walked the old man to the front door. As Jennings got into the car and the driver pulled away, Kelly turned and looked at Dalton. "Was he as helpful as you thought he would be?"

"He didn't tell me much more than what's in the public records, although I was surprised to learn that he'd once lived here." He raked a hand through his hair, his brow furrowed. "It's probably going to take several interviews with him to get all the information I want. I'm hoping that by talking with him I can make him remember things he might not have remembered at the time he helped write the Mesker book."

They walked back into the study where Dalton picked up his notebook and the tape recorder. "Thanks for letting me sit in and listen," she said. "I've always been fascinated by the whole story of Randolf and Daphne."

"What prompted your interest in them?" Dalton asked curiously. "I mean, most people our age don't even know who they were."

"Ah, but most people our age weren't raised by my grandmother." Kelly smiled. "She was probably the best fan your grandfather ever had. We lived not far from here, and often on Sunday afternoons we'd drive out here and picnic on the dunes down by the water. While we ate, she'd tell me story after story of the famous couple who'd once lived here.

"When I was fifteen years old she sat me down and made me watch one of Randolf's films." Kelly smiled at the memory, remembering that initial moment when she'd discovered the magic of the incomplete canvas a silent movie presented, where she could fill in the language, the dialogue, stretch her imagination to fill in the void. It had been at that same time that she'd discovered the power, the genius, of Randolf Weathers.

"Is that what made you decide to buy this place?"

Kelly nodded wistfully. "My grandmother didn't live long enough for me to save up the money I needed to buy it, but when she died she left me enough for a sizable down payment.'' She didn't tell him that there were times when she felt like her grandmother's spirit was right here in the house with her, sharing each experience, wrapping her in loving and supportive arms.

''Well, I guess I'd better get back upstairs and get this tape transcribed while the conversation's still fresh in my mind.'' He started to leave, then turned back. ''If you'd like to sit in on the rest of the interviews with Malcolm, you're more than welcome to.'' Although the words were gracious, his expression did nothing to either encourage or discourage her.

''Thanks.'' She smiled tentatively.

He nodded, and for a moment his gaze lingered on her. Intense, with a touch of boldness, it brought an immediate blush of heat to Kelly's cheeks. ''Good night, Kelly.''

''Good night,'' she murmured, watching as he turned and left the room. She immediately expelled a deep, shuddery breath. For just a moment—for just a single, solitary moment when he'd gazed at her—she'd felt the energy rippling off him, an energy that spoke of suppressed desire. But it was more than that, because for just a moment, that single, solitary moment, she'd felt an answering desire of her own.

Kelly stared out toward the water that retained the last of the sun's rays, her mind pleasantly numbed as she simply enjoyed the startling beauty of the ocean and the sunset before her.

In the past week everyone seemed to have settled into their new living arrangements with ease. Gary and Susan left early each morning, Gary for work and Susan for one of her many auditions. Jeffrey usually didn't make an appearance until after noon, when he took his easel and paints down to the beach. He spent more time snoozing on a blanket than he did painting, but he was quiet and polite and caused no trouble.

Kelly had seen little of Dalton in the past week. Malcolm had come for another interview and she had joined them, listening with interest to Malcolm's recollections of Randolf's early professional life. But that had been four days earlier and she hadn't seen Dalton at all since then. Twice, late at night, she'd heard the sound of a movie projector and so she knew he must be hard at work on his book.

Now she stretched her legs out before her and took a deep breath of the evening air. The sun's light on the water was slowly disappearing, as if each wave carried it farther and farther out to sea. She knew from experience that darkness would fall abruptly, leaving behind only the shimmering light of the moon to caress the ocean waves.

"Beautiful, isn't it?"

She jumped and turned around, smiling as she saw Dalton's approach. "Gorgeous. This is my favorite time of the day. There's something mysterious, almost magical, in the air at twilight."

"Mind if I join you?"

"Not at all." A flush of pleasure swept through her as she scooted over to give him room to sit beside her on the bench. She looked at him curiously and frowned, wondering what it was about him that seemed different. His resemblance to Randolf seemed even more striking than she'd noticed before.

"It's the mustache," he said, as if reading her mind. He reached up and touched the growth of whiskers that darkened the area above his mouth. "I got up the other morning and started to shave, then decided I'd try this. What do you think?"

"It's very attractive. It certainly makes you look more like your grandfather."

He looked out across the water, his hand reaching up once again to touch the faint mustache. "If only it could help me think like my grandfather," he observed softly.

"How's the book coming? I've heard the movie projector running late at night and figured you were burning the midnight oil, watching some of Randolf's old movies."

He frowned and looked at her quizzically. "That's odd, I haven't started looking at films yet. I haven't even unpacked the projector."

Kelly felt a ripple of unease creep up her spine. "How strange," she agreed. "I could have sworn I heard it."

"Not from my room."

She stared back out at the water, disturbed by his words. Twice in the past week she had awakened from a deep sleep, positive she heard the hum of the machine, the clicking of eight-millimeter film. She had immediately gone back to sleep, assuming the noise came from the attic rooms.

"Maybe your friend Susan has been watching old movies?" he suggested.

"Perhaps," she agreed slowly. Maybe he was right. Maybe Susan had been viewing old films to prepare for an audition. It made sense. Eagerly she accepted the logical explanation.

"Want to take a walk with me?" he asked, gesturing down the long expanse of beach.

"Okay," she agreed.

Together they rose and started down the sandy shore. "One night next summer I think I'm going to have an old-fashioned beach party," she said. "Complete with bonfire, music and fish baked over a pit. But in the meantime, I'm thinking of throwing a housewarming party."

"Sounds like fun," he agreed. "From all I've heard, Daphne always liked the house filled with people and often had parties." He looked at her, his dark eyes even more obsidian in the shadowed dusk of approaching night. "There's something I want to talk to you about."

"What?" Kelly carefully stepped over a large piece of driftwood, then looked at him curiously.

"Malcolm wanted me to ask you if you'd be interested in renting an apartment to him for the next three or four months."

"Sure, I've got the one on the first floor left," Kelly replied easily.

"He thought it would be easier for me to interview him if he was right here in the house, but he wasn't sure if you'd want to rent for just a couple of months. To tell the truth, I think the drive from his Manhattan penthouse to way out here for the interviews is perhaps too much for him."

"I'd love to have Malcolm here. I think he would be a wonderful addition. I had an ad all ready to call in to the paper advertising the apartment and now I won't have to call it in." Kelly smiled. "Oh, Grandmother would be so pleased. When she and I used to dream about owning this place and having little apartments, neither of us imagined not only Randolf's grandson would rent a room, but his agent as well."

They came to several sand dunes rising out of the beach. Kelly kicked at a piece of dried kelp, noting the stars overhead that twinkled their brilliance down to the water.

"This is where Grandma and I would come for our picnics," she said, easing herself down on the still-warm sand. "Sometimes we'd sit until long after dark, spinning fantasies of Randolf and Daphne's life together." She paused a moment, watching Dalton as he sat down next to her, then redirected her gaze to the house. "Grandma told me that, at least in the beginning, Randolf and Daphne had a sort of fairy-tale love."

Dalton followed her gaze toward the place where the two lovers had once lived and tragically died. "They were two passionate people. They loved each other with an intensity that shut out everyone else."

"I wonder what happened to make it all go so wrong?"

Dalton looked at her, the shadows of night clinging to his features, emphasizing the strength and sharply etched angles of his face. "That's what I want to do— go back and reconstruct their life together, see if I can pinpoint the moment when things started to fall apart. If he was truly mad and as evil as everyone said, then why did Daphne remain with him?"

"You said they loved each other passionately. Perhaps despite his mental instability she still saw a goodness in his soul," Kelly offered.

"Perhaps," he agreed without conviction. His eyes seemed to take on a new darkness and his jaw muscles tightened. "Or maybe she was seduced into staying with him by the very blackness of his soul."

"Is that what you believe?" Kelly asked softly.

"I don't know what I believe." He sighed in frustration and looked back at the house, seemingly drawn to it against his will. "Murder and madness. It's quite a legacy."

He stood up suddenly and brushed off the seat of his pants. "I think I'll get back to work." He turned and headed off, his form a dark, well-defined silhouette as he made his way across the beach.

Kelly watched him go, again wondering what dark forces drove him to explore a crime of passion that had occurred over fifty years ago.

Why not just leave it alone? Why not just get on with his own life? Question after question pounded in her brain, like the pounding of the water to the shoreline.

Why was it so important to him to prove that his grandfather wasn't an insane murderer? What Dalton's grandfather had done was certainly no reflection on who he was.

But Dalton seemed to have a special affinity for Randolf. Was it possible he was afraid that in some way he might make the same mistakes as his grandfather, might cause history to repeat itself and past tragedies to become present ones? Kelly shivered despite the unusual warmth of the evening air.

Had Randolf Weathers truly been crazy or had some catalyst driven him over the edge? And what kind of catalyst? Had it been something that would have driven any rational human being over the edge?

If Randolf had truly been insane, then she hoped Dalton could discover the reasons why... what had happened to push him into his madness. She had a feeling Dalton would never know peace until he understood what forces had driven his grandfather. He would never move on until he could somehow resolve the mysteries of the past. And if he couldn't, then that in itself would be the real tragedy.

She looked across the beach, squinting to see him in the night darkness. She finally spied him as he reached the back door.

As he disappeared through it, Kelly could have sworn all the lights in the house brightened a bit, as if welcoming his presence back within its walls.

CHAPTER FOUR

Kelly awoke suddenly, her heart beating an unsteady rhythm in her chest. She remained still for a long moment, wondering what it had been that had pulled her from her dreams.

The luminous hands on her clock told her it was a few minutes after midnight, and in the faint glow of moonlight, she could see that nothing was amiss in her room.

She closed her eyes, willing her heartbeats to a more even cadence. Then she heard it... just a whisper of sound so faint it could have been mistaken for her imagination or part of a dream. But she recognized it as the furtive sound of footsteps passing her doorway. Who was wandering the house in the middle of the night?

Her heart resumed its rapid thudding as she quietly swung her feet over the side of the bed to the floor. She grabbed the pale pink robe that was draped across the antique chaise lounge and pulled it on over her nightgown.

Unlocking her door, she opened it and stepped out into the darkened hallway. Standing motionless, she listened for any sounds, any indication that somebody was roaming around in the dark house. She took several steps, hesitating at the top of the staircase and peering down to the rooms below.

She thought she spied a faint glow of light coming from the study. Curious, she moved soundlessly down the stairs. She paused in the doorway of the study where the small lamp on top of the mahogany bar was lit, casting a small circle of illumination.

Dalton was there, his back to her as he studied the books on the shelves. For a moment she stood completely still, not alerting him of her presence, merely looking at him.

He was shirtless, his broad back looking eminently touchable in the pale light. As he reached for a book on one of the upper shelves, she saw the play of his muscles as they moved beneath his flesh, and she wondered how they would feel beneath her fingertips. She clenched her hands into fists, her fingers tingling as if they remembered the warmth, the strength, of his flesh. She shook her head to ward off the feeling of déjà vu.

"Couldn't sleep?" she asked softly.

He whirled around in surprise, relaxing as he saw her. "No. I haven't slept very well for the past couple of nights. I'm sorry if I woke you." He reached up and kneaded the back of his neck.

"Headache?"

He nodded. "Probably too many hours hunched over the computer keys."

"Ah, unfortunately one of the perils of the writing life." She smiled sympathetically, hesitated, then gestured to the love seat. "Come here and sit down."

He looked at her curiously, but did as she asked, sitting down on the love seat and watching as she moved around behind him. "I'm an expert at un-kinking neck and back muscles," she explained.

"If you can get rid of this headache, I'll be eternally grateful," he said, his voice deeper than usual, reflecting his pain.

Kelly smiled. "That won't be necessary. Just pay your rent on time and that'll be payment enough." She stood just behind him, eyeing his sleek upper back, able to visualize the knotted muscles beneath.

Her mouth suddenly dried and she realized the palms of her hands were slightly damp in anticipation of connecting with the broad expanse of bronzed skin.

Swallowing hard, she touched the back of his neck, moving her thumbs into the rich darkness of his hair, exerting small circles of pressure at the base of his scalp.

"Oh, that's wonderful," he breathed, dropping his head forward to allow her easier access.

Kelly moved her hands across his broad shoulders, kneading and working at the tight muscles with her fingertips.

There was a delicious intimacy in the act of massaging him, touching his warm skin and hearing his soft moans as her fingers worked their magic. It wasn't completely sexual, although the undercurrent was there, weaving a sensual bond between them.

She closed her eyes, feeling his energy transmitting through her fingertips. It was a white energy, clean and good. It wrapped around her, drawing her closer.

He leaned into her caress, settling deeper into the love seat, and she could feel the muscles unknotting, relaxing their coiled tenseness.

"Your friend Susan mentioned to me the other day that you do computer work," he said, the words almost slurred by his sheer exhaustion.

"I write programs, mostly accounting and book-keeping. There have been many times when Susan's massaged *my* shoulders because of too many hours at the computer."

"I guess I didn't realize just how tense I've been." She could hear in his tone that slowly the tension was starting to ebb and he was finding his way to the floating, peaceful state of complete relaxation.

"Shh, just relax," she whispered, giving him permission to sit quietly and accept the gift of the massage.

Kelly didn't know how long she stood there, working her fingers into his muscles, enjoying the feel of his warm, firm skin. A scent of mint soap and maleness emanated from him and she breathed deeply, enjoying the tantalizing combination. She could tell by Dalton's breathing that he was, if not completely asleep, teetering on the edge.

Around them the house was silent, embracing them in a still, middle-of-the-night hush that seemed almost magical. Kelly could almost imagine Daphne doing this same thing for Randolf—massaging away the day's tensions, enjoying the feel of his skin beneath her fingers.

Reluctantly she dropped her hands and stepped back, smiling as he didn't move a muscle, didn't raise his head. He was asleep, soundly, peacefully.

She moved around in front of him, for a moment merely gazing at him, wondering exactly what it was about him that attracted her. Granted, he was very handsome, but her fascination with him extended further than mere physical attraction.

There was something about him that reached inside and stroked her soul, as if the energy she felt vibrating from him was a silken thread that found a part of her inner being and swaddled it. Despite the fact that she found something about him daunting, almost forbidding, there was an equally strong pull directing her toward him.

She smiled ruefully, realizing the lateness of the hour and her own fanciful imagination were combining to create crazy thoughts.

She gazed at him, hating to wake him up, but knowing he'd have new kinks in his neck and back if she left him to sleep on the small love seat.

She reached forward to touch him, but hesitated, straightening as an odd scent assailed her nose. Fragrant and stoking a strangely nostalgic note within her, the odor filled the room. Bay rum. She suddenly identified the smell, remembering it from years earlier when her grandfather had splashed it on every morning after shaving.

She looked around the room, trying to discern the source. She hadn't smelled it before. Maybe Dalton had been wearing it and the warmth of the massage had made it radiate more strongly.

Once again she reached toward him and this time she gently touched him on the shoulder to awaken him. His eyes instantly flew open, black and wild, staring at her without focus. Immediately Kelly felt a cold current glide through her, squeezing her heart and surrounding her in a void where the only emotions she felt were utter hopelessness and despair.

Energy radiated from Dalton's eyes, a dark, simmering power, and they seemed a caldron of bitterness and anger. Hatred—a black evilness—boiled there.

Kelly gasped and stepped back, frightened by the intensity of the force of his gaze. Then he blinked, and the look was gone, confusion and disorientation in its place. "I . . . I'm sorry, I must have fallen asleep." He sat up and experimentally rolled his head in a circle. "You should patent those massages."

"I—I'm glad you're feeling better," Kelly stammered, wondering if she'd only imagined the momentary soulless gaze in his eyes.

He stood up and smiled at her, the first real smile she'd ever seen from him. The warm intimacy that had lingered between them earlier was back once again. "Thanks for the massage." Even his tone of voice held a soft intimacy that was provocative. He took a step toward her. His eyes darkened, but this time Kelly felt no fear. She felt a like response as she recognized the emotion in his eyes.

He didn't embrace her, didn't lift his arms from his sides at all. He merely leaned forward and touched her lips with his own, the very gentleness of the kiss shaking her more than anything else he could have done. As he withdrew his mouth from hers, he gazed into her eyes and she felt as if he'd reached inside and stroked the surface of her heart. "Good night, Kelly," he said softly, then left the room.

As she crossed the room to turn out the lamp, her body trembled inwardly, whether from the effect of his kiss or the frightening power of that momentary blackness in his eyes, she wasn't sure.

Kelly stood in the doorway of the study, watching her housemates mingling and conversing. "Malcolm, more tea?" she asked, moving over to where the old man sat near the fireplace.

"That would be nice. Thank you, my dear."

Kelly refilled his cup, then set the teapot back on the coffee table.

"You know dear, you have certain gestures that remind me of Daphne," Malcolm observed, stirring his tea thoughtfully. "For instance, the way you just poured the tea. Daphne used to hold the pot just like that when she'd pour. And there's a certain way you hold your head when you're listening—" He broke off with a gentle smile. "Ah well, it's probably nothing more than wistful thinking on my part. There are times I still miss them both dreadfully."

Kelly touched the old man's shoulder and smiled, then excused herself. Looking around, seeing that everyone seemed satisfied, she left the study and went into the kitchen to get the bowl of dip and some potato chips.

Malcolm had moved into the house earlier in the day, and this evening Kelly had invited everyone to the study for an impromptu party.

So far the evening had been enjoyable. The conversation had flowed effortlessly from topic to topic. Even Jeffrey had joined in, animatedly debating politics with Gary.

"Can I help?"

She turned to see Dalton standing in the doorway. She flushed with pleasure. She'd hardly seen him since his good-night kiss the night before and she had no control over the way her heart raced at the sight of him. "Sure, you can carry in that tray of cheese and crackers." She gestured to the tray on the countertop. "Did you sleep better last night?" she asked, ripping open the bag of chips and pouring them into a large bowl.

"Definitely, thanks to you. You could make a fortune if you bottled those massages and sold them." He smiled wryly, his gaze lingering on her. "But then again, I'm not sure I'd want just anyone feeling your fingers on their back."

Kelly's flush deepened. She realized there was a new familiarity in his tone, a familiarity and a strange sort of possessiveness. It thrilled her on one level, and sent off tiny warning signals on another. "I've heard your grandfather could be a charming man," she answered lightly. "I guess you not only inherited his dashing looks, but his charm as well."

A cloud of darkness eclipsed his smile. "Let's hope that's all of my grandfather's personality I inherited," he mumbled, more to himself than to her.

Kelly suddenly realized the burden the past placed on him. Perhaps Gary was wrong. Maybe the past really did have the power to affect the present and direct the future. She placed a hand on Dalton's arm. "You are not your grandfather," she said firmly, definitely.

His smile darkened. He reached out and stroked gently down the side of her cheek with his thumb. "No, I'm not. But if my grandfather was truly insane, then the same blood runs through my veins." His hand fell back down to his side and his mouth twisted in vivid frustration. "And if he wasn't insane and he didn't kill Daphne, then himself, then *who* killed them?"

"Find the truth and write your book," Kelly replied, once again feeling his darkness surrounding her. She hesitated a moment, looking deep into his eyes. There were secrets there, and passion, and the driving force of a man on a mission she wasn't sure she understood.

"There are times," she began tentatively, "times when I'm sure I can feel the presence of something in this house...something unsettled...like restless spirits of haunted souls." She laughed self-consciously and moved away from him. "You probably think I'm crazy."

His dark eyebrows shot up in amusement. "Coming from my dubious background, I'd say I have little room to judge anyone as crazy or sane."

"Hey, Kelly, did you get lost in here or what?" Susan poked her head into the kitchen. "We were wondering where you two snuck off to."

Dalton frowned at the intrusion and picked up the platter of cheese and crackers. "We were just getting some food," he explained.

"We're coming right now," Kelly said and, grabbing the chips and dip, she followed Susan and Dalton to the study. "Would anyone like another drink?" Kelly asked moments later as she stepped behind the small bar.

"I'd love another Scotch and soda," Susan said from her perch on the love seat.

"That sounds good to me," Gary agreed.

"Dalton?" Kelly looked at him expectantly.

He shook his head. "Nothing for me." He held up his glass. "I'm still nursing my club soda."

"Obviously not a drinking man," Malcolm observed, nodding in approval at Dalton. "The tendency toward alcoholism is inherited. With Randolf's background there's no point in you taking a risk. Alcohol can be a dreadful demon when it possesses you."

Dalton merely nodded, a jaw muscle pulsing ominously in the side of his face.

As Kelly fixed the drinks, she was relieved to hear Malcolm and Dalton go on to talk about the house, their voices socially pleasant, although Dalton's held an undercurrent of tension that never seemed to go away.

"Randolf had the house built," Malcolm was explaining. "He was out here every day supervising the workmen, changing the plans, adding his own bits of genius."

"Kelly showed me the stairway that leads up to nowhere," Dalton said.

"A stairway that leads nowhere?" Jeffrey looked at Kelly quizzically.

"The stairs are in a closet. You open the door and they go up toward the roof, but just stop at a dead end," Kelly explained.

"Awesome!" Jeffrey exclaimed.

Malcolm shrugged. "Who knows exactly what Randolf had in mind with the stairs. Perhaps he intended to add another room, then changed his mind."

"There's also a hidden passageway," Kelly said, sitting down on the floor next to Malcolm's chair.

"You never told me that," Susan said accusingly. "Where is it?"

Kelly felt her face warm slightly. "It runs from the bookshelves in my room to the attic room."

"My room?" Dalton looked at her in surprise. "But where? I haven't noticed a doorway."

"In the back of your pantry closet. The carpenters who renovated found it."

"Awesome," Jeffrey repeated. "This Randolf dude must have been some guy."

"I still say it's too bad these walls can't speak," Susan observed. "Imagine the stories they could tell us."

"Maybe they *could* tell us," Jeffrey said, his blue eyes shining with youthful eagerness. "We should hold a séance, see what kind of spirits we can get to talk to us."

"Uh-uh, not me," Susan protested. "The last thing I want to be involved in is a séance in a house where a woman was murdered by her crazy husband." She grimaced and flashed an apologetic look at Dalton. "Sorry."

He nodded, indicating no offense was taken.

Malcolm smiled at Jeffrey. "Séances and ghosts...a bunch of nonsense if you ask me."

"Then you don't believe in ghosts?" Kelly asked.

"Certainly not," Malcolm returned. "I've lived a long life, seen many strange things, but my experiences have all been of this world."

"I'm with you," Gary replied, agreeing with the older man. "Ghosts are nothing more than the wistful longing of people left behind who refuse to allow the dead to remain dead."

Kelly thought about this. She remembered the times since her grandmother's death that she'd thought she felt the old woman's spirit wrapping around her, comforting her with warmth and love. Were these sensations only products of her mind, things she imagined because she couldn't face the reality of her grandmother's death?

"I don't know about that," Jeffrey said dubiously, voicing Kelly's own sentiments. "I think it's possible that sometimes people on the other side of life can't let go, can't move on until they settle up any unfinished business."

"Yes, I've heard the speculation that if a person dies a sudden or violent death, they are disoriented and don't pass on, but linger in some sort of transitional plane." Malcolm shook his head with a small smile. "If that was truly the case, then Daphne and Randolf should be banging doors and rattling chains, because they certainly fit the notion of people who suffered violent, unexpected deaths."

"Daphne died violently and unexpectedly, but if the stories are true, Randolf took his own life," Dalton reminded the group.

"Well, then, tell me, Kelly. Have you had any female spirits walking around the house, causing mischief?" Malcolm asked with an indulgent grin.

"No, at least not that I'm aware of," Kelly answered with a touch of hesitancy. No, there was nothing specific she could put her finger on, no doors opening and closing by themselves, no unearthly cries in the night.

But there *was* something here . . . an energy, a force that whispered in the darkened hours of the night, swelled the walls of the house with a pulsating tremor only she seemed to feel.

"The sight of a ghost rattling a chain in my face will send us straight out of this house and back to our tacky little Manhattan apartment," Susan exclaimed, pulling Kelly from her thoughts. "I'm sorry, Kelly. You're my best friend, but I won't brave an unhappy dead person for anyone."

Malcolm laughed. "My dear, I don't think you have to worry about anything. The dead are just that—dead."

At that moment soot exploded out of the fireplace, hanging in the air for just a moment before settling on the throw rug.

Susan squealed and jumped out of her chair, and Gary cursed soundly, brushing a thin layer of the dark ash off his arm.

"It must have been some freak downdraft," Kelly exclaimed, rushing to the fireplace and reaching up to shut the flue. She turned back around to face the others and for just a moment got a whiff of the distinctive scent of bay rum.

"I guess the dead don't like to be called dead." Susan laughed, but her laughter held an edge of nervousness.

Malcolm brushed off his jacket. "It would take a lot more than a little wind down a chimney to make me believe in ghosts." He eased himself forward in the chair. "And as lovely as this little soiree has been, I'm afraid I'll be dead if I don't get these old bones to bed." He stood up and smiled at everyone. "I think this living arrangement is going to be just splendid." With a gracious nod and another smile, he left the study.

Malcolm's departure seemed to be the impetus for everyone to call it a night. Once they had all left, Kelly quickly picked up the dirty dishes and washed them in the kitchen sink. As she worked, a smile curved her lips. It had been a pleasant evening. Malcolm had been charming, talking about the glory of old Hollywood, the magic of Broadway. Even Jeffrey had gotten into the spirit, shedding his usual awkward shyness to ask questions of the old man.

The smile wavered slightly as she thought of Dalton. Although he'd been sociable with everyone, he'd kept an emotional distance from them all.

He confused her, and frightened her just a little bit. She sensed a core of goodness inside him, but it was tinged around the edges with a blackness she couldn't understand. Yes, he confused her, attracted her on a gut level, yet he also repelled her in a nebulous way. Only at the moment, the attraction far outweighed any other emotion.

She put the last of the dishes in the drainer and shut off the kitchen light. Returning to the study, she straightened the flower arrangement in the center of the coffee table, then crossed the room to turn out the lamp. As her hand reached for the switch, she noticed a figure standing on the patio just outside the back door.

Dalton. She'd thought he'd gone to his apartment when the others had left, but he'd apparently stepped outside instead.

He stood with his back to her, wearing the heavy cloak of darkness the night provided. She approached the doorway, wondering what he was doing. He stood without moving, as if in deep concentration, and she wondered whether she should bother him or not.

If he didn't want to be bothered, then surely he would have gone to his room, she thought. "Dalton?" she called his name softly through the barrier of the screen door. He didn't move and she wondered if he'd heard her.

She opened the screen door with a noisy creak, but still he didn't move, didn't flinch or turn his head. As she stepped outside, she was immediately embraced by cold air wrapping fingers of ice around her. It wasn't the usual cool night air blowing in off the water. This was something different ... frightening....

"Dalton." She heard the urgency in her own voice as she called to him again, felt an inexplicable fear that caused her heart to pound in an uneven tempo. Whether that fear was of him or for him, she couldn't tell. She only knew that there was danger in the icy air.

What frightened her as much as anything was his obliviousness to her presence. Although they stood only a few feet apart, he seemed to be in another place, a place where she couldn't reach him.

She leaned over and touched his shoulder. Cold. It was as if she stood in a deep freeze and she could feel the arctic air surrounding him, as well, enveloping his flesh. "Dalton ... for God's sakes," she exclaimed, giving his shoulder a shake.

Her breath caught in her throat as she saw a vaporous mist suddenly seem to rise out of the top of his head. Like a cloud of steam, it was a hazy gray in color and seemed to glow with an energy of its own. At first without form or definition, it coalesced, expanding and pulsating until it resembled an almost human form. But then, as quickly as it had appeared, it was gone, evaporating into the thick night air that surrounded them.

For a long moment Kelly didn't move. She *couldn't* move. Her mind raced, desperately trying to explain what had just happened, what she'd thought she'd just seen. "Dalton..." His name released itself from her mouth, no more than a croak.

He turned immediately and smiled, his brow wrinkled with vague confusion. "Kelly. I didn't hear you come out."

"I...I..." She stared at him, moved closer and realized the unnatural cold dampness was gone. The air smelled of the ocean and the breeze was cool, but not unusually so. Did she imagine it? she wondered wildly. Had it been the moonlight reflecting off a low cloud floating across the sky and her mind had somehow perceived it as erupting out of the top of his head? It had to have been a trick of the moonlight, an illusion somehow produced by something completely natural. Didn't it?

"Kelly? Is something wrong?" He reached out a hand and touched her arm, the warmth of his fingers somehow reassuring her.

"No...no, I'm fine." She brushed a hand across her eyes, as if to remove any cobwebs that might have tricked her. "I guess I'm just overtired."

He stepped closer to her, bringing with him the seductive scent she'd noticed the night before. "It was nice of you to arrange this little party to welcome Malcolm," he observed.

"It should make it easier on you having him right here whenever you want to talk to him," she said, acutely conscious that he hadn't removed his hand from her arm.

"Yes, it will be convenient." His eyes glittered darkly as he gazed at her and his fingers softly caressed her skin.

Again Kelly felt her breath catch in her throat, but this time it wasn't due to fear. He stood so close, his breath fanned against her face.

It would be easy to fall into the dark depths of his eyes, lose herself in the mysterious abyss they held. Again she felt the simmering potency of tightly contained emotions emanating from him and she found herself wanting him to lose control, wanting him to swallow her up in a blackness so complete she couldn't think, but could only feel.

"Kelly." He spoke her name softly, as if he, too, didn't understand the overwhelming force pulling them together like the very gravity that held them in place.

She knew he was going to kiss her. She also knew it would not be a kiss as gentle, as unassuming, as the one he had given her the night before. She welcomed it, tilting her head back, knowing her invitation was in her eyes and on her lips.

He wrapped his arms around her and pulled her tightly against the length of his body, letting her know that he was aroused.

When his lips touched hers, they weren't soft and gentle, they were hot and hungry, stealing her breath away and causing her heart to thud almost painfully hard against her rib cage.

She had thought she could easily lose herself in the depths of his eyes, but she felt her sense of self slipping away beneath the sheer eroticism of his kiss.

He tasted of the sand and the sea, of hot winds and black starless nights. The sensation of his body touching hers so intimately only served to heighten her response, evoking in her a need to melt against him, meld with him.

His lips burned a path to her heart, his tongue stealing the secrets of her soul. Energy pulsated around her and through her, and she couldn't figure out if it was black or white, good or bad...and she didn't care. She only knew that with his kiss he'd taken a part of her and claimed it as his own.

He pulled away from her, a dark smile lifting one corner of his mouth. "Oh, Kelly, you'd be a most tempting diversion in another place and time." He reached out and traced her jawline with the tip of his finger, the touch sending flames of fire licking at her insides. "But I can't afford a diversion at this time in my life." He frowned and dropped his hand. "And I think I'd better get upstairs and back to work on the book before temptation wins over good sense." Without waiting for her reply, he turned and disappeared into the house.

When he was gone, Kelly wrapped her arms around herself and shivered slightly, remembering that moment when his lips had possessed hers. It might have lasted only a moment, or it could have lasted a lifetime, for the element of time itself had slipped away as his lips had plundered hers.

At that moment he'd owned her, body and soul. Had he pulled her down to the concrete and taken her against the gravelly surface, she wouldn't have had the will to resist.

It was frightening, the utter domination he'd had over her in that single instant in time. She'd never experienced anything like it before. Yes, it was frightening, yet it was also seductively thrilling.

She stared out onto the dark water, which was barely discernible in the blackness of the night. She frowned, something niggling at the back of her brain.

Looking around, she had the feeling that something wasn't quite right. Something was definitely wrong, but she couldn't quite put her finger on what bothered her. What was it? What was wrong?

Then she realized what it was. There was no moon. She looked upward, seeking the glow of the lunar light. But the moon, the stars, the very heavens above were obscured by a thick layer of black clouds.

She began shivering again, the tremors not caused by memories of his kiss, but by the thought of the vaporlike fog she'd thought she'd seen escaping from his head.

She'd rationalized that what she'd seen had been a strange reflection of the moon on a cloud. But there was no moon. So what had she seen?

CHAPTER FIVE

Kelly walked along the beach, her thoughts focused on Dalton and the kiss they had shared the night before. Despite the fact that it was just after noon, the day was gray, the sun hidden with a thick haze of clouds that smelled of approaching rain.

She'd slept restlessly, tossing and turning, trying to rationalize away both the effect of Dalton's kiss on her and the strange apparitionlike mist she'd seen coming out of his head. It had looked so odd, and the sight had filled her with such a strange sense of anxiety.

It was nearly morning before she finally reasoned herself into believing that it had been nothing more than a trick of nature...a fog bank or a low cloud that had only appeared to rise from him. Nothing else made any kind of sense at all.

Her response to his kiss was more difficult to rationalize. It had been swift, insane, completely unexpected.

In her twenty-seven years, there had been a few men in her life and she'd certainly been kissed many times before. Still, no kiss had even begun to grip her as intensely as Dalton's had.

In that single moment when their lips had met, she'd relinquished all control of herself, lost touch with reality, been vulnerable as never before. It had been both wonderful and frightening.

She believed that neither she nor Dalton were in complete control of the overwhelming attraction between them, that the phantom winds of fate had blown them together and destiny had a secret plan for them.

What that plan was and where it might lead, she had no idea, but she had a feeling that they were helpless to fight against it.

She smiled, pushing her disturbing thoughts aside as she saw Jeffrey just ahead. He was completely absorbed in the canvas he was painting, his tongue caught between his teeth in complete concentration.

He looked up at her approach, a shy smile lifting his lips as he waved his paintbrush in greeting.

"How's it going?" Kelly asked.

"Not bad," Jeffrey answered, "although I prefer to be out here when the sun is shining and I can work on my tan as I paint."

Kelly smiled. "If every day was a sunny day, the world would be a pretty boring place. We need the cloudy ones so we appreciate the sunny ones."

Jeffrey nodded, his long hair flopping over one eye. He shoved it aside with the back of his arm. "I've finished, wanna see?" He gestured to the canvas where he had been working.

"May I?" she asked hesitantly. He nodded affirmatively, and Kelly moved around so she could see the painting he'd been working on. She looked in surprise at the canvas, her breath catching in her throat.

The scene was of the beach and the house in the distance. There was a touch of the surreal to the painting—the house appeared to breathe, and the beach seemed to writhe, as if attempting to escape the house that sat upon its sand. It was achingly beautiful and more than a little disturbing.

"Oh, Jeffrey...it's wonderful," she exclaimed, surprised by his obvious talent.

"You can have it," he said, again with a shy smile that lighted his boyish features.

"Oh no, I couldn't," Kelly protested, touched by his offer.

"Really, I'd like for you to have it," he insisted. He took the canvas by one corner and held it out to her. "Just be careful, some of the paint isn't dry yet."

Kelly hesitated, then nodded. "I'd be honored to own it, but would you sign it for me?"

He flushed with pleasure and placed it back on the easel. Dabbing a tiny brush into the black paint, he added a jaunty *J* in the lower right-hand corner, then carefully handed the painting back to her.

"Thank you, Jeffrey. I'll always treasure it. Someday when you're rich and famous, I'll have the satisfaction of telling people you began your illustrious career right here in my home and on this very stretch of beach." She could tell her words pleased him immensely. His face blushed bright red and he kicked at the sand. "Well, I'll let you get back to work," she said. "Again, thank you."

As she walked away, she looked back, seeing that he'd placed an empty canvas on the easel and was already at work on another painting. She looked down at the picture she held, again amazed by his obvious talent. Perhaps someday he *would* find fame and fortune as an artist. She hoped so. He was a nice kid.

She took the painting into her room and set it on her table, then poured herself a glass of iced tea. Carrying it with her, she left her apartment and went down to the large, empty living room. She'd worked most of the morning finishing up a computer program and had decided to take the afternoon and strip off the last of the old wallpaper in this room.

Using a spray bottle of vinegar and warm water, and armed with several putty knives, she set to work. She worked diligently, keeping her mind consciously numb, at peace with the silence of the house around her. She knew both Gary and Susan had left earlier in the day. No sounds came from Malcolm's apartment and she assumed he was probably taking a nap, and Dalton was probably busy with his research at his computer.

Dalton... She shoved thoughts of him out of her mind. She didn't want to think anymore about him. The kiss they had shared had stirred her beyond reason, but he'd made it clear he wasn't looking for a relationship. He wanted his complete energy and concentration on his book. That suited her just fine. She wasn't looking for a relationship with a moody writer who radiated a strange energy, an inner torment. Especially one who would finish his project and then move on.

She scraped energetically at a stubborn piece of paper, thinking of the floral pattern she wanted in the room. She'd found a picture of this room in an old movie magazine and she'd studied it until the pages had worn thin.

Daphne had decorated the room in tones of deep purple and dark green, the wallpaper patterned with tiny sprigs of violets. Kelly had searched and searched and finally found the paper she wanted, a close match to what had once decorated the walls.

She paused in her scraping, hearing the sound of water dripping down drainpipes. Looking out the window, she realized the heavy gray clouds were delivering their promise of rain.

She heard the slam of the back door, then the closing of another door, and knew Jeffrey had returned to the house, probably cursing Mother Nature soundly for ruining his outside activity.

The house loved the rain, gurgling in pleasure as the water ran down the drainpipes and pattered against the windows. Unlike the storm that had raced across the sky earlier in the week, there was no thunder to detract from the soothing rhythm of the rain, no lightning to break the embracing grayness.

She didn't know how long she'd been working when she finally stepped back and looked at the results, her arm exhausted and aching from her exertions.

She'd accomplished a lot. Another day of work would probably finish the last of the stripping. She set the spray bottle down and turned around, gasping in surprise as she saw Dalton standing in the doorway.

"Oh, you startled me," she exclaimed. She felt a blush heat her cheeks as she wondered how long he'd been standing there watching her.

"I'm sorry, I didn't want to interrupt your work." He stepped into the room, immediately filling it with his presence. He looked distracted, his hair wild, as if he'd raked his hands through it many times. "Would you mind looking at a couple of things for me?" He held out a sheaf of papers.

"Not at all," she agreed, wiping her hand on her jeans and taking the papers from him. "What am I looking at?"

"Old gossip clippings from various sources. I've noticed something they all have in common and I'm wondering if I'm losing my objectivity or if there's really something odd there."

She frowned, not sure she understood what he wanted or what she should look for. She sat down on the floor, crossing her denim-clad legs beneath her, and spread the sheets of paper out.

She was acutely conscious of him joining her, easing himself down on the floor next to her. She focused her concentration on the papers, scanning each article quickly. There were pictures of Randolf and Daphne having a meal at Maxim's, the two of them attending a theater opening. There were small paragraphs and full pages about the famous couple.

She finally looked at Dalton, a frown furrowing her brow. "I don't understand...."

"Look." He rearranged the clippings, making two piles. "These—" he gestured to one stack "—are clippings of gossip items that appeared before Randolf and Daphne's deaths. And these—" he pointed to the other pile "—were all written after their deaths."

Kelly looked at the articles again, this time more carefully, but whatever it was that he wanted her to see still eluded her. She could feel Dalton's frustration rolling off him in waves, but finally she admitted defeat. "Dalton, if there's something specific you want me to find in these, you're going to have to give me something more to go on."

He sighed and ran a hand through his dark hair, his eyes glittering with intensity and keen intelligence. "Maybe it's nothing," he said with a sigh. "Maybe I *am* grasping at straws."

"Dalton, just tell me what it is you think you've found," Kelly exclaimed impatiently.

He stared down at the clippings for a long moment, then looked back at her. "In all the articles written while Randolf and Daphne were alive, there is absolutely no hint of Randolf being an alcoholic...no report on him drinking excessively on any occasion. Yet the articles all written after his death quote a close source and talk about what a drunk he was. It just seems strange, inconsistent."

"And you think the close source is Malcolm," she guessed.

He shrugged his shoulders. "Who else? He was their best friend, Randolf's agent." His frown deepened. "I just can't understand how a man as public as

Randolf could exhibit such restraint when in the public eye, yet be a raving drunk in his private life."

"Malcolm is probably the only one who would have the answer to that. You should ask him."

"I intend to," he said succinctly. Then he continued, "In fact, I'm meeting with him in the study in a half hour for another interview. You're welcome to sit in."

"I'd like to," she agreed, helping him gather up the papers on the floor.

"I also ran across this." He handed her a folder. "It's an old script," he said as she opened it up and read the title.

"*Silent Screams*. It certainly sounds intriguing."

"Hmm, but what *I* find intriguing is that this was sent to Randolf a year before his death, when he was in the midst of his career slump. Here—" he pointed to a note scribbled in faded pencil at the top of the first page "—is a note from the director. He says he's sent a copy of the script to Malcolm and he really hopes Randolf will agree to do the movie. What I can't figure out is why he didn't do this movie. I read it—it looks like a sound script."

Kelly shrugged. "I guess Malcolm will have that answer, too. Could I read this?" she asked, then grinned. "I've never read a script before."

"Sure." He stood and extended a hand to help her up. The moment she took his hand, she felt the coiled heat of desire flare inside her. It took her by surprise, caused her to stumble against him, and as she bumped into his chest, she saw the flare of an answering desire in the darkness of his eyes.

She stepped away from him, wanting to distance herself from the invading warmth that boiled inside of her, but the physical distance did no good. His eyes reached out to her, embracing her in their hot liquid, beckoning her to plunge into the flames. She felt herself drowning in fire, engulfed in heat as moments passed and their gazes remained locked.

He finally broke the gaze, taking a few steps backward as if he, too, felt and fought against an overwhelmingly magnetic pull. Kelly felt his energy, hot and wild, pulsating and dangerous. "I'd better get my things ready for the interview with Malcolm," he said, then turned and left.

Kelly's breath escaped out of her in one long whoosh, making her realize it had been trapped somewhere inside her for several long moments.

There was something about Dalton that scared her, but her fear was all tangled up with desire, the two emotions creating an emotional battleground inside her.

She'd be smart to ignore the feelings he evoked inside her. She'd be smart to stay away from him, forget their shared kiss, fight against getting involved with him on a more personal level.

But even as she thought this, her body rebelled, remembering the sensation of his lips against hers, the feel of his body pressed intimately against her own, his potent eroticism that threatened to carry her to a place she'd never been. She didn't know if she had the power to fight the dark magic that radiated from him. And she wasn't sure she really wanted to.

She put her tools away and cleared up the wallpaper she'd stripped off, then went back to her own apartment and got into the shower.

As she stood beneath the hot water, her thoughts were consumed with Dalton. He would only be here at the house for the duration of his literary work. Once his book was finished he'd go back to his life in New York City. She'd be a fool to get involved with him, knew that if she did it would be a brief, but emotionally devastating, kind of affair.

The minute he'd arrived here he'd filled the entire house with his presence. The restless, frustrated energy that radiated from him was so powerful, it frightened Kelly. Yet she couldn't ignore the magnetic pull that existed between them. It went deeper than physical attraction, was more powerful than any mere chemical reaction.

She tipped her head back, letting the water cascade down her throat and breasts, her entire body tingling as she remembered the power and lingering memory of his kisses.

There was a darkness inside him, a darkness of such magnitude it threatened not only him but everyone around him. She didn't know what caused it or where it came from; she only knew the evocative pull it possessed, a pull that called to something equally powerful inside her.

She shook her head and plunged it beneath the stream of water, wondering if she was only imagining things. She had never before been so affected by a man. Perhaps Dalton was merely making her face a well of sexuality she didn't know existed inside her. Maybe that was what frightened her. Not any strange power in him, not any answering power in her... just good old hormones racing in a way they'd never raced before. Yes, surely this explanation made better sense than anything else.

She got out of the shower, feeling somewhat better. She dressed in a pair of jeans and a checkered cotton blouse. Despite her resolve to stay away from Dalton, her interest in his interview with Malcolm was much stronger.

She didn't have to get involved with Dalton to listen to the interviews, she rationalized as she left her apartment and went downstairs toward the study.

They had already begun. As she approached the study door, she heard the low murmur of Malcolm's voice and the deeper, answering tones of Dalton. She paused a moment just outside the door, wondering if she should interrupt them. At that moment, however, there was a lull in their conversation and she stepped inside.

"Ah, good evening, Kelly." Malcolm smiled his delight at her appearance.

"Good evening, Malcolm," she returned, nodding at Dalton. "I hope you don't mind if I join you?"

"Certainly not. There's only one thing an antique agent loves more than discovering a new talent, and that's an audience when he tells stories of his past."

"Malcolm was just telling me how Randolf was cast in the lead role of *Splendid Obsessions*," Dalton explained as Kelly sat on the love seat across from the chairs where the two men sat.

"That was his first film, right?" Kelly looked at Malcolm, who nodded vigorously.

"Indeed, his first film and the one that shot him to the heights of stardom. It took me months to convince the studio powers that he was worth the gamble. They weren't too excited about casting an unknown." Malcolm settled back in his chair and entwined his fingers. "I convinced them to give him a screen test, then I financed the trip to California. By that time Randolf and Daphne had just married and they were financially destitute."

"So you took Randolf to California for his screen test and the rest is history," Dalton observed.

"History... yes. Randolf was magnificent. The studio people talked for months afterward about his screen test." Malcolm cocked his head to one side and gazed at Dalton. "Really, it's amazing how much you remind me of Randolf. Not only physically, but you seem to have much of the same sort of emotional character as well, that simmering passion just beneath the surface. Anyway," he continued, "after the screen test, there was no stopping Randolf. For the next several years, everything was wonderful. Randolf was on the top, Daphne got pregnant and gave birth to your mother, and the money was rolling in."

"Why did they decide to build this house here? Why not in California where so much of Randolf's work was?" Dalton asked curiously.

"Both Randolf and Daphne insisted they wanted their home here. They didn't want to live in Hollywood, didn't want to get caught up in the Hollywood games." Malcolm sighed heavily. "By the time Randolf began building this place, the darkness in his soul was starting to be apparent."

Dalton leaned forward, his features taut with tension as he focused all his attention on the old man. "What do you mean—the darkness of his soul?"

"By the time I moved in here with them, just after the house was built, Randolf was suffering horrible hallucinations." Malcolm frowned thoughtfully. "The hallucinations were the initial signs of his madness."

"What kind of hallucinations?" Dalton asked.

Malcolm shrugged. "He never told us the specifics, but they must have been horrible." Malcolm's gaze was distant. "Soon after that was when his temper became so black. He was drinking heavily, although he usually denied it, and he would get so angry that I grew afraid for Daphne." His gnarled hands trembled slightly in his lap. "His possessiveness with her grew daily, and I tried to get her to leave. I told her he was insane, but she insisted it was just the stress he'd been under. By that time his career had hit the skids and stories were circulating of his instability."

"I'd like to talk a little bit about his drinking...." Dalton pulled out the newspaper articles he'd shown Kelly earlier. "I've pored over these newspaper and magazine stories and there's one inconsistency that puzzles me. There is not a single account that mentions Randolf's alcoholism while he was alive. It's only in the articles following his death that alcohol is even mentioned at all."

"And you find that intriguing?" Malcolm laughed. "I find it a testimony of my attempts at damage control. When Randolf was alive, the last thing I wanted was for anyone to discover he was a heavy drinker. I paid off many a reporter to make sure stories of his overindulgence didn't reach print. After his death, it didn't matter."

"What about *Silent Screams?*" Dalton asked.

Malcolm looked at him blankly. "I beg your pardon?"

"It was a movie. I found the script in a box of things my mother had. Apparently the director of the movie desperately wanted Randolf for the lead."

"Ah yes, I seem to remember that particular project. I didn't think it was right for Randolf."

"Not right?" There was suppressed anger in Dalton's tone. "Perhaps in doing that film Randolf would have proved to everyone that he still had the same star quality that made him famous in silent films. It would have been his vehicle into talking films."

Malcolm eyed Dalton with a touch of wry amusement. "Dalton, my boy, I have the feeling you're reaching—trying to blame my management tactics for your grandparents' demise, searching for anything that will somehow vindicate your grandfather from blame. I'm afraid you will be sadly disappointed. You can reach all you want, but the truth is Randolf was evil and crazy, and he shoved the woman he loved down the stairs, then went and got a gun and shot her and himself.''

He stood up and rubbed a hand across his forehead. "Randolf was like a brother to me, and the most difficult thing I ever had to admit to myself was that he was evil. He had a blackness in his soul that eventually destroyed his goodness. And I have a feeling you won't know any peace until you admit that to yourself.'' Again he rubbed his hand across his brow. "Now, I'm afraid I must stop for tonight. This delving into the past wearies me." With a nod at both Dalton and Kelly, he left the study.

For a long moment neither Kelly nor Dalton spoke. She felt his enormous frustration as it filled the room. He got up off the sofa and moved to stand at the back door, his posture rigid with tension.

"Dalton?" She stood up and walked over to stand just behind him. She reached out a hand, then clenched it into a fist and withdrew it before touching him. Something about his stance forbade her making any physical contact with him.

"I know there's more to it than just a senseless act of madness," he said, his words taut with suppressed emotion. "I know there was something else at work here. My grandfather was not insane or evil. Something else happened that night. I know it as surely as I'm standing here."

"Isn't it possible you feel that way because you want it so badly?" Kelly ventured.

He whirled around and glared at her, his eyes as dark, as fathomless, as the pits of hell. A bitter laugh erupted out of him, one filled with such torture, it moved Kelly back a step. "God, I wish it were as simple as that, but it's not...it's something worse." He reached up and put his hands on either side of his head as if trying to suppress something horrible. "For the last six months there's been a force at work, a dreadful force that I can't fight, compelling me to research Randolf and Daphne's death, whispering to me that something is wrong—dreadfully wrong—with the official accounts."

He released his head and instead gripped her by the shoulders, his fingers digging painfully into her tender flesh. "I wish it was just my need to clear my grandfather's name, but it's more than that. It's become an obsession that I'm no longer in control of...a domination that I can't fight."

"Dalton...please...you're hurting me." She squirmed beneath the strength of his fingers. He immediately released his grip and stumbled backward from her.

"I need...I need some fresh air." Without waiting for her reply, he whirled around and disappeared out the door and into the descending darkness of night.

Kelly moved over to the doorway, her hands rubbing at her shoulders where his fingers had pressed. She'd probably be bruised.

As she massaged the tender areas, her gaze sought him out, a solitary figure heading toward the water. The rain had stopped sometime earlier, but the wind blew, ruffling his hair as he made his way to the ocean's edge. She shivered and wrapped her arms tightly around her body, noting how all the deepening shadows of the approaching night seemed to seek him out, cling to him like a shroud.

She shivered again and turned away. Slowly, thoughtfully, she made her way to her rooms. There was a small part of her that was frightened of Dalton, and a small part that was frightened *for* him.

Was he battling the torment of personal demons? Or was there something more ominous at work? He'd spoken of the force that drove him as if it had nothing to do with him, as if it was an entity entirely separate.

She undressed quickly and slipped on her nightgown, the cool silk soothing against her skin. She turned out all the lights but one, a floor lamp that sat next to the luxurious chaise lounge. She grabbed a book by the bed and stretched out on the lounge, deciding she would read for a little while, then go back downstairs and check to make sure Dalton was back in the house.

She would never be able to sleep if she didn't make certain the outside doors were locked. Although each tenant had their own key to those doors, she had no idea if Dalton had his with him when he'd stormed outside.

She curled up on the satin-covered chaise and opened the book. It wasn't until she realized she'd read the first line four times and still didn't comprehend the words that she knew her concentration wasn't up to the task of reading. She slammed it shut and leaned her head back, her hand stroking the cool material that covered the chaise.

The chaise lounge was one of the few pieces of furniture that had come with the house. Originally, it was mildewed and water-stained, and Kelly had spent a small fortune to have it re-covered. However, it had been worth it; the chaise had become her favorite area of rest and thought. She always felt somehow closer to the original owners of the house when she was lying in the chaise.

She jumped as a soft knock rapped at her door. She hurried to answer, pulling on the matching floor-length silk robe to her nightgown. She opened the door, stepping back in surprise as Dalton swept past her and into the room. She pulled her robe more tightly around her and faced him.

He smelled of the recent rain, a wild, earthy scent mingling with the subtle odor of his spicy cologne.

"I've come to apologize," he said, pacing the room like a caged animal. "I didn't mean to frighten you earlier." He frowned and raked his hand through his wind-tossed hair. "I . . . I just want you to understand that this book I'm writing, the whole process of digging up the facts about Randolf and Daphne's deaths, it's not just a whimsical notion for me. It's not just some literary project to pursue. I know it sounds crazy, but I feel as if I was driven to come here, led by the passions and mysteries that surround my grandparents' deaths."

He walked toward her, his eyes as black as night as they caught her and effectively pinned her in their intensity.

"This house is so filled with their spirits." His voice was a soft whisper, was an evocative warmth on her face, and in the darkness of his eyes she saw a flame ignite. "I feel them in the middle of the night, hear them in the creaks and groans of the house. The overwhelming passion they felt for each other is all around us. Can't you feel their passion?"

He stood so close to her his lips were mere inches from hers, and the heat from his body torched through her. "Don't you feel it, Kelly?"

Once again he placed his hands on her shoulders. This time his touch wasn't painful, but hot through the thin cool silk of her gown and robe, mesmerizing in its soft caress.

She hesitated a moment, feeling herself being pulled into the flames that now lit the very center of his pupils. She wanted to protest, deny, fight against the falling sensation, fight against the hypnotic power of his very presence. But then she felt the ageless passions engulfing her, overwhelming her, and she knew Dalton was here to follow through on the restless energy, the intense sexual desire, that had pulsated between them for the past several days. "Yes," she whispered, and with that single acknowledgment, she knew she was lost.

CHAPTER SIX

Dalton pulled her toward him, his mouth immediately seeking hers in a kiss that stole her breath away. His lips plied hers with fevered heat as his arms encircled her and pulled her closer. His tongue gently teased its way between her lips, flicking against hers in hot demand...exploring...searching...seeking all her mysteries.

He tasted of the rain and the wildness of the sea, filling her senses with a pleasure that both numbed and drugged her.

She had no opportunity to erect defenses, no chance to build any guard against the invading sensuality of his kiss. Her sensibilities slipped away, overpowered by the sheer, all-consuming authority of his mouth.

He broke the kiss only long enough to move his lips down her jawline, raining hot, eager kisses as he whispered her name over and over again.

His body pressed intimately against hers, his hips urging in primitive command. His hands caressed slowly down her back with mesmerizing results.

Kelly felt as if she'd been plunged into a pool of thick, dark liquid. She dropped her head back in acquiescence, knowing somewhere in the depths of her mind that she should resist, but unable, or unwilling, to exert the effort to swim herself up to the surface of sanity.

She opened her eyes, her vision blurred by the depths of passion that stirred within her. She was conscious of their silhouette on the wall, a shadow of two melding into one. The sight only further stimulated her desire.

She frowned, watching as the silhouette appeared, then disappeared. She suddenly became aware of the lamp next to them flickering off and on, as if the light bulb wasn't properly inserted. It blinked on and off a number of times, then remained off. The only light in the room was the occasional lightning of another approaching storm that drifted in through the windows. But it was enough that, as Dalton raised his head and looked at her, she could see perfectly the unmasked hunger in his eyes.

Kelly stared at him, slightly disoriented as she realized in the darkened room that it was easy to imagine him as Randolf, and herself as Daphne. The passions of the past that once had existed between the two now swirled around them. Like mists of fog, it pulled them deeper and deeper beneath its hold, whisking them to a place where there was no time, no identity, nothing but the obsessive need they had for each other.

In one smooth movement, he picked her up in his arms and carried her toward the bed. She didn't resist; in fact, she welcomed the strength of his arms, then the feel of the solid mattress beneath her.

His mouth once again found hers, claiming her lips with fiery intent, and she felt the last of her conscious thoughts winging away. With a soft sigh, she gave herself to him, returning his kiss with a white heat of her own.

His hands moved across the silken material of her robe, parting it and removing it, revealing the thin gown beneath. His mouth moved down her throat, lingering at the areas on her shoulders where his fingers had pressed painfully before.

She gasped as his lips moved on, capturing one of her nipples through the material of her gown, his breath transforming the cool fabric to heated silk. The sensation made her mindless, and she tangled her hands in the thickness of his hair, wanting to pull him closer, against her, into her.

With a soft groan, he pushed the straps of her gown down her shoulders, then sat up and slowly pulled the gown down her body, leaving her only in the matching tiny floral silk panties. For a moment he remained sitting, merely staring at her. His gaze was as potent as a touch, causing liquid fire to lick at her insides.

Still holding her gaze, he stood up and pulled his shirt off, exposing the strength and symmetry of his broad chest. He unbuttoned his jeans and stepped out of them, splendidly naked in the vivid lightning that rent the room.

Kelly moaned her pleasure as he came to her once again, lying on top of her, moving against her, his dark chest hair rubbing erotically against her breasts.

"Kelly... Kelly..." He spoke her name softly as he kissed her cheeks, her eyelids, capturing her mouth with fervor. The soft hair of his mustache added to the erotic pleasure of his lips on hers.

Her hands loved the smooth skin of his back, the compelling strength of his shoulders. She loved the hot pressure of him so intimately against her, which spoke of his consuming passion.

"Dalton," she breathed, arching up to press against his bold desire, letting him know she wanted him, needed him.

One of his hands glided across her breasts, down the flatness of her stomach, to cup her feminine warmth, stroking her softly through the silky, wispy panties.

Her breath caught in her chest at the exquisite sensation his touch evoked. Wanting to return the pleasure, she reached down and took him in her hand, stroking him with light caresses that made him growl deep in his throat.

He removed her panties with trembling hands, poised above her for an eternity as his gaze sought hers. When he finally took her, he became the moon and the stars, swirling her into a velvet fog of sensation. She was Daphne and Kelly, and all that was feminine, and he was Randolf and Dalton and all that was masculine.

He loved her slowly, thoroughly, completely, taking her to the edge again and again, only to withdraw and withhold complete satiation until she feared she would explode.

Then he moved faster, his body setting the rhythm, and Kelly matched it, until she reached her peak, clinging to him as her senses shattered into a million pieces. She was vaguely conscious of him stiffening against her, hoarsely calling her name.

Suddenly she was surrounded by an intense white energy and knew his soul touched hers as he rode the crest with her and hoarsely called her name one last time.

Afterward she remained cradled in his arms, awed by their lovemaking and the intense emotions he'd evoked in her. She shivered slightly, remembering that single moment when she'd felt surrounded by the brilliance of his soul. In that instant she'd have sworn the entire room sizzled and snapped with blue arcs of electricity.

Had she only imagined it? She shivered again.

His arms tightened around her, pulling her against his warmth. She felt she should say something, but didn't want her voice to break the spell of magic that cocooned them together. She allowed her body to relax against his and slowly drifted off to sleep.

She awoke suddenly. Cold. Icy cold. Dalton lay on his back, soundly sleeping as a storm overhead vented its fury. Vivid lightning slashed the room's darkness, and thunder crashed, seeming to shake the very foundation of the house.

She lay there for a moment, her body bathed in an arctic chill that penetrated through the blankets and into her very soul.

The window must be open, she thought, groaning at the vision of leaving the bed to fix the problem. But she was freezing and knew she wouldn't be able to go back to sleep until she closed it.

Reluctantly she slid out of bed, goose bumps dancing on her arms as the full brunt of the cold air danced across her naked skin. She hurried to the window and threw back the curtains, surprised to discover the window was tightly closed. In fact, the temperature of the air next to the window was cool, but not unpleasantly so.

Confused, she hurried to the bed, once again surrounded by the strange, frigid air. There seemed to be a pocket of the wintry temperature around the bed.

As she got back in beneath the blankets, Dalton stirred, mumbling something unintelligible in his sleep. Then a flash of lightning lit the room, and she saw his features twisted in torment, as if he was suffering from a horrible dream.

She scooted over closer to him and placed a hand on his shoulder. She drew it back immediately as she felt his cold skin. The chill seemed to emanate directly from him.

"Dalton." She touched his shoulder once again, repressing a shudder of revulsion at the corpselike temperature of his flesh. "Dalton, wake up."

His eyes fluttered, and immediately the air around them warmed. He opened his eyes, staring at her for a long moment. Then he smiled. "Ah, Daphne," he whispered softly and pulled her into his arms, trapping her against his slowly warming flesh.

* * *

Dalton awoke with the first light of dawn creeping into the window. For a long moment he remained unmoving, enjoying the warmth of Kelly's body against him, the scent of her that surrounded him.

The inner torment that had tortured him, driven him, controlled him for the past six months was momentarily silent, and he savored the peace, knowing it was only a fleeting respite.

He hadn't intended for this to happen. He hadn't wanted to get either physically or emotionally involved with her. And now he was both.

He gazed at her. Even in sleep she was lovely. She looked so fragile, with her slender shoulders exposed above the blankets and her lashes casting shadows beneath her eyes. Yet, he had a feeling she had a fierce inner strength, and it was this strength that drew him. He tightened his arm around her, watching as her eyelids fluttered like butterfly wings, then opened.

For a swift moment, the blue of her eyes clouded with confusion, then they cleared and she smiled, a soft smile that crawled into his heart. "Good morning," she murmured, the husky morning voice causing his blood to course more rapidly through his veins. He immediately felt his physical response as she stretched languidly, like a cat, the blanket falling to expose her full breasts.

"Good morning," he replied, propping himself on one elbow, then leaning forward to capture a rosy nipple between his lips.

"This is crazy," she gasped, her hand tangling in his hair as a moan of pleasure escaped her.

And it was. It was all crazy, a madness, he thought as he stroked her body, felt the way she opened herself to him both physically and emotionally. Despite his resolve to stay away from her, keep his energies focused on the book that demanded so much of him, from the moment he'd stepped into the house Kelly had exerted a pull on him he couldn't deny.

Where the obsession with the murder of his grandparents was powerful, a black kind of madness that controlled him, this enormous attraction to Kelly seemed to be his sanity, the only thing good and right.

As she wrapped her silky legs around him, pulling him closer, deeper into the craziness, he let his thoughts drift away and gave himself completely to the act of making love to her.

Afterward, they showered together, not speaking of what they had shared or where they were going, only enjoying the soft silly talk of lovers.

"Take a walk with me on the beach," he suggested when they were once again dressed.

She nodded, again giving him the smile that sent a shaft of emotion through him.

The early morning sun shimmered on the water, painting the waves in golds and pinks. Gulls cried overhead, diving down into the breaking waves for their breakfast.

They walked to the place in the sand where Kelly and her grandmother had once picnicked, sitting down on the night-cooled sand. The breeze off the water had dried the top layer of the sand, and other than the pieces of debris brought in by the waves, there was little remnant of the storm that had passed in the night.

Kelly picked up a handful of the sand, allowing it to sift through her fingers, her gaze surreptitiously studying Dalton as he stared back at the house. "Regrets?" she asked with a false lightness.

He shook his head. "No. How could I regret something so beautiful? Although I have to admit, you weren't exactly in my plans when I first arrived." As if with an effort, he pulled his gaze to her. "Kelly, I don't know where we're going to go from here."

"We don't have to know," she said softly. "We can just take it one day at a time." She frowned, noting his features once again possessed the tension, the darkness she'd noticed so many times before. "What?" She reached out and touched his arm. "What is it, Dalton?"

"I don't know. I feel a horrible sense of foreboding. I've felt it ever since moving in." He was still looking at the house, his eyes haunted. "Since my mother's death a year ago, thoughts of Randolf and Daphne have absolutely consumed me."

"It was a horrible tragedy," Kelly said.

"It consumed my mother, as well. She suffered nightmares all her life, nightmares of that night. She knew that her father couldn't have been responsible for Daphne's death or his own." His hands clenched into the sand at his sides. "But trying to figure out what exactly happened is as difficult as trying to capture a grain of sand in a wind storm. There are times I think I'll go as mad as Randolf.''

Kelly gripped his arm firmly. "I won't let that happen," she exclaimed.

He smiled, and for a moment the darkness ebbed and the shining light of his soul surrounded her. "You'd fight my demons for me?"

Kelly nodded. "That's me—landlord, computer expert, lover and warrior against all demons."

He laughed. The first laugh Kelly had ever heard from him, and the deep, resounding sound sent waves of warmth sweeping through her. The laughter faded and he studied her with an intensity that brought a heated blush to her face. "You need to realize I'm obsessive about my work. I sit at the computer for hours on end and hate to be interrupted."

"Then I know not to interrupt."

"I drink too much coffee and keep strange hours."

"Then it's a good thing you have your own room," she returned smoothly. She felt him reaching out to her, needing her, but she wasn't sure exactly what it was he wanted.

He nodded, then hesitated a long moment. "There's a darkness in me I don't understand, a darkness that seems to grow daily. I can't seem to fight it or push it away. Until I get past this obsessive need to write my grandparents' story, I can't make any promises."

"One day at a time, Dalton," Kelly repeated. "I wasn't exactly expecting you in my life, either. But something is working between us. I don't know what it is or where it came from. But I'm willing to see it through, see where it leads." She looked at him curiously.

"So am I," he said, the darkness once again momentarily swept away. He leaned over and touched his lips to hers, then stood up and brushed off the seat of his jeans. "I guess I'll get back to work."

He held out a hand, but she shook her head. "I think I'll just stay out here for a little while longer."

"I'll see you later this evening?"

She nodded, watching as he made his way back to the house. She knew she should feel some sort of guilt. After all, it had been only yesterday when she'd determined she'd be a fool to get involved with him. Still, she couldn't regret what had happened. She felt an inevitability had pulled them to this place and time, the same force that had driven him to this house in the first place.

She also knew that, despite the darkness she sensed surrounding him, he had a core of goodness that was pure and strong. Smiling, she remembered that single moment when she'd felt them unite spiritually as well as physically. Was that how it had been for Daphne and Randolf? Had their love transcended mere physical and emotional levels? Had their souls entwined to create a love obsessive enough to result in a tragedy?

She shoved these thoughts out of her mind. Dalton was *not* Randolf and she certainly wasn't Daphne. She frowned as she remembered waking him up in the night, how his arms had tightened around her and he'd whispered Daphne's name. And the coldness of the room . . . it had been an unnatural temperature, seeming to radiate from his skin.

Still, with the warm morning sun shining warmth on her shoulders, her body still tingling with the pleasurable memory of Dalton's touch, it was impossible to hold on to these thoughts. Surely it had been nothing more than a draft in the room, and it was only natural that Dalton might whisper Daphne's name in his sleep. He was spending all his waking hours researching the woman's life.

She raised her face to the heat of the sun, a smile returning to her lips. A party, she thought suddenly, deciding to follow through on her idea of a house-warming party. It would be a perfect opportunity to show off the house and also introduce her renters to the people in the area.

Mentally she began assembling a guest list. All the doctors she'd written computer programs for and some of her grandmother's friends. Then there was the nice reporter who'd written an article about her when she'd first bought the house and decided to renovate it. She'd send out the invitations in the next day or two and plan the party for three weeks' time.

This settled in her mind, she stood up and brushed off the seat of her pants, her thoughts drifting again to Dalton. The thought of their lovemaking filled her inside with a heat more intense than that radiating from the sun. But as she approached the house and reflected on his talk of the inner darkness that plagued him, the obscure power the past held on him, she felt a sudden shiver of apprehension.

She paused and gazed up at the looming structure of Randolf's house and felt an ominous foreboding sensation, wondering if it was the same one Dalton had spoken of only moments before.

The warmth that had suffused her suddenly dissipated, leaving behind a fist of cold that had no logic, and that squeezed her heart.

CHAPTER SEVEN

The shimmer of pale light drifting in through the porthole window broke Dalton's intense concentration. He frowned, pushed away from his computer and walked over to peer outside. Dawn lit the eastern skies, causing him to look at his wristwatch in disbelief.

Where had the night gone? The last time he'd looked at his watch it had been nearly 8:00 p.m. He'd decided at that time he'd work for another hour, then go down and spend time with Kelly. His concentration on his work had been so intense the hour had apparently expanded and he hadn't realized the night had disappeared.

He stifled a yawn with the back of his hand and turned away from the window. Coffee...he needed fresh coffee, and maybe a brisk, early morning run on the beach.

While the coffee dripped through the machine, he changed into a pair of jogging pants and a sweatshirt. Within minutes he hit the sand. Despite the chilliness of the early morning, it didn't take him long to break into a sweat. Gulls squawked overhead, as if protesting his presence on the deserted beach. Waves lapped greedily at the shore, creating a thunderous rhythm he matched with his jogging.

It frightened him a little bit, how easily the night had slipped away without his noticing. He'd written two previous books, both works of fiction, but never had he gotten so engrossed in his work that he lost large chunks of time in the process.

Obsession. It wasn't a strong enough word to describe what he felt about this particular book. When a person was obsessed, they were usually in control, they owned their emotions. But Dalton had a feeling he wasn't in control of this. He was being led by a power far greater than mere obsession.

He shook his head and slowed his pace, his troubling thoughts replaced by reflections of Kelly. Strange how just thinking about her created a sort of glowing inner peace. From the moment he'd seen her, he'd been pulled toward her, captivated by her beauty, intrigued by her intelligence, attracted by the inner strength that radiated from her.

One thing was certain. He and Kelly couldn't go backward, couldn't take back what they had shared. There was no way he could look at her and not remember the taste of her lips, the satiny texture of her skin, and the way, at the moment of climax, their souls had made contact and conversed.

A connection had been forged, one that he knew would not be easily broken. It was a connection stronger than time, more powerful than the past, and he realized there was an inevitability, a sense of rightness in their being together.

He jogged back toward the house, a smile lifting his lips. He'd told her yesterday that he'd see her last night. Instead he'd written all night and she hadn't interrupted him. She'd taken him at his word that he didn't like interruptions, and she'd respected his work time. He'd go inside, have a shower and a cup of coffee, then he'd find her.

Once inside, he took a quick shower, poured himself a cup of coffee and was about to leave the room when he realized he must have left the computer on. He sat down at the table and stared at the computer screen, where all the work he'd done last night was displayed. Gibberish. It was all gibberish.

He scanned down screen after screen of the pages he'd written, a fascinated horror sweeping over him as he saw the nonsensical words and sentences that comprised his night of work. What had happened? Perhaps a glitch in the hard drive? Through some electronic oddity had all his files been turned to gibberish? Surely not.

He pulled up file after file, relief sweeping through him as he saw that they all seemed to be okay. It was only his previous night's work that was ruined. He finished his cup of coffee, then poured himself another, walking around the room and trying to figure out what had happened. Had he spent the entire night typing in gobbledygook?

He threw himself back down in the chair in front of the computer, focusing his concentration on the screen filled with random letters that made no sense. As he stared, the letters seemed to shimmer, then swim around the screen. In fascination he watched as the letters danced and wiggled like bugs on a screen door.

I'm too tired, he thought, downing the coffee as if it was a shot of whiskey. He squeezed his eyes and rubbed his fingers across them. He could feel his heart not only beating in his chest, but throughout his entire body, pulsating with an unnatural severity.

Slowly he opened his eyes and gazed back at the computer screen. The type bounced out of the screen and onto the floor, leaving the glowing computer screen blank...void of anything. In horror he shoved away from the table and stood up, the floor tilting beneath his feet like the deck of a storm-tossed ship.

What was going on? *What was wrong with him?* He flailed his arms wildly for balance, then clutched at the wall, immediately drawing back as it moved beneath his fingertips. He backed away, hearing the pounding of his heart like a loud echo that reverberated throughout the entire room. He stared at the wall, which had transformed into a sea of worms, writhing gray creatures with smiling, happy faces.

"No." The word tore from his throat and he stumbled to the window and peered out the glass. He was able to see his own reflection in the pane. It laughed at him, the sound exploding all around him.

Seeking safety in a place suddenly alien and frightening, he crawled up in the center of the bed, staring around him in a sort of fascinated horror. The walls exploded with color, vines and flowers grew, then withered and dropped to the floor.

The ceiling above had become a sky of turbulence. Dark clouds swirled around his head and lightning flashed in the corners. He smelled the flowers, their scent heavy and pungent, then the odor of sulfur filled his nose. He grimaced in distaste, seeking reality but unable to find it in the horror landscape that surrounded him.

The door floated open and Kelly came in, her hair a cascade of vines, her face a mere skeleton. "No," he moaned, reaching out a hand to the macabre figure. Malcolm was also there, laughing as he danced around the room with an agility that belied his age. Jeffrey stood in the corner painting obscene graffiti on the walls.

God. He clutched his head between his hands and closed his eyes. What was happening? Dear God... what was happening? Even with his eyes closed he could hear the room breathing, sighing, moving with a life all its own. He heard giggling, evil, malevolent laughing, but he didn't open his eyes. He didn't want to see the source of the sound.

Afraid as he'd never been in his entire life, he curled up into a fetal ball.

Kelly sat on the stone bench on the back porch, addressing invitations for the housewarming party. She'd been disappointed when she hadn't seen Dalton the night before, but knew he'd probably been absorbed in his work. She had the feeling that the darkness she sensed surrounding Dalton would eventually be dispelled with the writing of his book. Somehow, in coming to terms with the deaths of his grandparents, he would exorcise the dark demons that haunted him.

"Ah, here you are."

Kelly turned to see Susan approach her. "I knocked on your door but you didn't answer," Susan said, sitting down next to Kelly on the bench.

"Here I am." Kelly grinned at her friend. "No auditions today?"

Susan shook her head. "Although I've got to go into the city this afternoon. I'm meeting a woman at our apartment to see if she wants to sublet. Gary will be a much happier camper if we can get rid of that extra payment."

Kelly frowned. "Maybe you guys should have waited to move in here until you had the other place rented."

"Nah, we didn't want to wait. Gary has been much more satisfied and less stressed not having to ride the train an hour to work in the mornings. It's worth the little bit of financial strain." Susan tucked a strand of her hair behind her ear and gazed out at the beach. "Besides, we didn't have a view like this in the city."

For a moment the two sat silently, enjoying the view of the water rolling into the sandy shore. The sun sparkled brilliantly on the tops of the waves, making them appear to be diamond-tipped.

"So, what are you working on?" Susan asked, gesturing to the invitations in Kelly's lap.

"I'm having a party... a housewarming party."

"Sounds like fun. When?"

"Three weeks from now. The first Saturday in October. It will take me that long to finish up the work in the living room."

"Count me in for any help you might need. You know me, the original party animal." Susan stood up and looked at her wristwatch. "Well, guess I'll head up and shower. If I leave here early enough I can get in an hour of shopping before I have to be at the apartment." Wiggling three fingers, Susan disappeared into the house.

Kelly watched her go, then stared back out at the beach, a smile curving her lips upward as she remembered some of the parties she and Susan had attended when in college. While Kelly had always lingered on the fringes of any party, more observer than participant, Susan had been the very life of any get-together, dancing on tabletops, chugging beer with the guys, singing ribald songs that made everyone laugh.

Susan was a good friend, one with whom Kelly had always been able to share her innermost secrets. But she hadn't wanted to share with Susan her newfound relationship with Dalton. It was too new, too special to share with anyone for the moment.

Now she looked up at the tiny porthole window of his room, wondering what he was doing. Was he thinking of her? Remembering their lovemaking, the bond that had been created?

As she stared at the window, a face suddenly appeared behind the pane of glass. Her breath caught in her throat at the horrifying sight.

It was there only a moment, then gone. But even when the window was once again empty, the momentary vision remained etched in her mind.

It had been Dalton, wide-eyed, his hair wildly tousled, his mouth open as if in a silent scream. He'd looked exactly like Randolf. *He'd looked completely insane.*

For a long moment Kelly didn't move, couldn't tear her gaze from the window where Dalton had been momentarily framed. She held her breath, wondering if he would appear again, hoping that her impression of him had been wrong.

He'd looked so bizarre, so…crazy. She wrapped her arms around herself, suddenly aware of the coolness of the wind, the chill taking up residency deep within her.

I'm the one who's crazy, she scoffed inwardly, shoving her sense of disquiet aside. She'd seen only a flash of him, an image probably distorted by distance and light.

Still, she suddenly felt the need to go to him, check that everything was all right. Surely he wouldn't mind just a brief interruption of his work.

She got up and went inside, placing the invitations on her bed. She crept silently up the stairs and paused outside his door. She raised her hand to knock, but hesitated, listening to the quiet on the other side.

Although there was something inside her encouraging her to check on him, make sure he was okay, the silence told her differently. If something was really wrong, wouldn't she hear something?

Her hand, poised to knock, fell back to her side. She was suddenly reluctant to disturb him, worried that perhaps her own motives weren't so clear. Was it genuine worry that made her seek a connection with him, or was it merely a need prompted by their night of lovemaking? Would he see her interruption as concern or some sort of pathetic need?

With a sigh, she turned and made her way back downstairs, entering her room just as the phone rang. It was one of the doctors she had written a computer program for. They were having a glitch with the program and wondered if she could come right over and see what she could do to fix it. She told them she would, hung up and grabbed her purse and car keys.

She'd probably see Dalton this evening, she thought as she got into her car. One day at a time, she reminded herself. He'd warned her that he was obsessive about his work, often spent long hours at the computer.

She was gone for most of the afternoon. The computer glitch was in the program and it took her several hours of work to correct the problem. After leaving the doctor's office she did some shopping, picking up groceries and discovering a lamp to put in the living room when the wallpaper was completed.

As she drove home, her thoughts once again drifted to Dalton. It was difficult to believe how quickly he'd gotten under her skin, into her heart. Yet when she remembered how he'd affected her the moment he'd stepped out of the rain and into her kitchen, she wasn't so surprised. Almost immediately there had been an intense attraction, an attraction more profound than mere physical desire. It was as if a strange, magnetic force had drawn them together like two clouds colliding and had then created an electric energy between them that snapped and popped.

The same intensity that guided his search for answers to his grandparents' deaths, he'd brought with him to their lovemaking. The result had been a searing memory she knew would be difficult to forget.

She thought about that moment when her bedside lamp had blinked rapidly several times, then remained off. She also remembered that first night she'd taken him up to his room. On that night the lights had been erratic, too.

Gripping the steering wheel more firmly in her hands, she replayed in her mind the night she'd thought she'd seen the vaporous mist rising from him, that moment when she'd been unable to make contact with him despite the fact that he stood mere inches from her.

She shivered slightly, realizing that despite her enormous attraction to him, in spite of the fact that he'd made love to her gently, tenderly, there was still a small part of her that was somehow afraid of him.

The air in the car suddenly seemed cold, and she reached over and switched the heat on, grateful when warm air began blowing from the vents.

Her grandmother would have told her to quit "feeling" so much and use her head rather than her senses. Although her grandmother had usually encouraged use of her special gift of sensitivity, she had also prompted Kelly not to rely on it, to temper it with intellectual reasoning.

And intellect told Kelly there was nothing more amiss than her overworked imagination and the fact that Dalton possessed a stronger intensity than anyone she'd ever known before.

She'd told him she'd battle his darkness, be a warrior against his demons. But she had a feeling his inner darkness was powerful.

She shoved her troubling thoughts aside as she pulled up before the house. Funny, how she always referred to it as *the* house, or Randolf's house, she thought. She paused before getting out of the car, taking a moment to simply stare at the place. Early evening shadows sought the cracks and hollows of the structure, contrasting with the glow of the last gasp of day that lingered with a golden hue.

An unusual uneasiness crept over her, as dark as the ebony hues now capturing the house. The shadows seemed darker than usual, more ominous, creating a pall of gray that engulfed the entire structure.

"I'm being silly," she chided herself, as if, with her voice alone, she could break the spell of apprehension. Still, she couldn't shake the feeling that something alien was in the house, something dark and menacing—watching . . . waiting.

With a dismissive shake of her head, she got out of the car and went inside. The shadows that had clung to the exterior of the house crept inside, darkening the entry hall with pale gray fingers.

She carried her groceries to her room, noting the utter silence surrounding her. It was an eerie silence, as if the house held its breath in anticipation. There was no noise from any of the other rooms, making it seem as if she was the only person in the house and the others had been swept up and carried away.

She put her groceries where they belonged, trying to shake the foreboding that gnawed inside her. She ate a light supper, then grabbed a paperback book she'd been reading in spare moments and went down to the study. When Dalton finally surfaced from his work he would find her here.

Curling up on the love seat, she leaned her head back and opened the book. Within minutes she was engrossed in the fictional story unfolding on the printed pages....

She jerked suddenly and opened her eyes, instantly aware that she had fallen asleep. She must have slept for some time because the room was filled with darkness, the only illumination coming from the moonlight spilling in through the window.

She remained still, waiting for the sleep-fog to clear from her mind. It was then she heard it . . . the clicking sound of film through an old projector.

The sound seemed distorted, as if it traveled through a distant space and time to reach her. She assumed the noise came from Dalton's room, but as she listened intently she realized the noise didn't come from above her, but rather surrounded her.

It was like listening to an old-time melody, the haunting tones of a harpsichord playing a half-remembered song. It wrapped around her, enveloping her in a misty haze, obliterating her sense of time and space.

She closed her eyes again, feeling the sound drift around her, through her. It was easy to imagine that the present had slipped away, stolen by the rhythmic clicking of the antique machine. It was easy to imagine that Randolf was upstairs, watching old reels of himself, analyzing how to make his next performance more brilliant. And more than that, it was easy to imagine that she was Daphne, and she loved the man upstairs with an intensity that transcended time, that exceeded life and death. She frowned. But was it a love that had endured despite murder?

Once again she opened her eyes, sensing a presence nearby. She sat up on the love seat, trying to pierce the nearly impenetrable darkness of the room. Something was there. She felt it. She jumped, startled as she saw a looming, opaque shadow in the doorway. Her heart jumped into her throat, making it impossible for anything more than a gasp to escape.

CHAPTER EIGHT

"Kelly?"

She expelled a shuddery breath of relief. "Jeez, Dalton, you scared me to death." She got up and made her way across the room to turn on the lamp on top of the bar. She turned back around, the smile on her face wavering as she looked at him in shock. "Dalton... are you all right?"

His hair was wild, as wild as his eyes, which appeared wide and haunted. A pallor covered his face, making the blackness of his eyes deeper than midnight, ebony wells of anguish.

He leaned heavily against the doorframe, as if afraid that without its solidity he would fall. He looked exhausted... defeated... haunted.

"Dalton?" She hurried to him, placing a hand on his arm, surprised at the fevered heat of his skin.

"I'm—I'm all right." As if with an enormous effort, he pulled her against him, holding her tightly, almost desperately. "I'm all right," he repeated, this time more forcefully. "I just had a bad afternoon, the flu or something... exhaustion." He pulled her with him toward the love seat, where they both sat down.

"Should I call a doctor or something?" Kelly asked, eyeing him worriedly. He didn't look good at all. She berated herself for not following through on her instincts earlier in the day. She'd felt that he'd needed her, and she'd ignored those feelings.

"No, I'm feeling better." And he was. The hallucinations had seemed to last forever. He'd finally fallen asleep and when he'd awakened a few minutes ago, they were gone.

But the memory of those horrifying visions lingered in his head, and the possibility of what had caused them swelled his heart with horror.

When he'd first seen Kelly, he'd felt an overwhelming relief. In his visions her hair had been snakelike vines, her grin had been that of a skeleton. When she'd turned on the lamp, he'd been relieved to see she was back to normal. He'd hugged her close, needing to touch her reality, reassure himself that he really was better.

Now, with the warmth of the study surrounding him and Kelly's sweet scent enveloping him, he did feel better. But he couldn't shake the horrifying dread that twisted inside him.

"Dalton, are you sure you're all right?" Her gaze lingered on him worriedly, and he nodded. Physically he was feeling better, but emotionally he was a wreck.

He ran a hand over his brow. He didn't want her to know what he'd experienced that afternoon, yet he felt like he would go truly mad if he didn't talk about it to somebody.

A part of him wanted to gather her into his arms and repeat their earlier electric experience. Perhaps if she held him close enough, tightly enough, it would purge the fear that ate at him. But another part of him was afraid, afraid of pulling her into the darkness with him. He sighed, too tired, too weak, to sort it all out at the moment.

"I stayed up all night, got so involved in my research I didn't realize the night had passed." He ran a hand over his eyes. They felt gritty with exhaustion. "I went for a short run on the beach and when I went back into the room, I sort of hallucinated." He looked at her, waiting for an expression—any expression—to cross her features, but she merely returned his gaze calmly.

"What do you mean you sort of hallucinated?" she asked.

He looked into the azure blue of her eyes, so trusting, so giving, and he suddenly didn't want to tell her any more. "Never mind," he said, rubbing at his eyes once again. "It was just a bad afternoon and I shouldn't have gone so long without sleep. I think what I need most right now is to go back to bed," he finally murmured.

"Wait.... What kind of hallucinations?" she pressed.

He tensed, thinking of the frightening visions he'd suffered. A shudder vibrated through him. "I—I don't want to go into it now," he said, standing up from the love seat. "I just need to get some rest."

"That's probably a good idea," she said sympathetically. "You might be fighting off a flu bug or something. You do feel rather feverish." She walked with him to the doorway of the study. "Are you sure you can make it up the stairs?"

He nodded, pausing a moment to look at her. She was so lovely, and if he allowed himself he knew he could very easily fall in love with her. But he wouldn't allow himself. He couldn't. Not now.

He turned and started up the stairs. No, he couldn't get any more involved with Kelly. He was afraid for her. He was afraid for himself.

His hand trembled on the banister as he remembered what he'd gone through all afternoon. The images had been so horrible. They had seemed so real.

Was it his destiny to follow his grandfather's trek into insanity? An insanity that ended the life of the woman he cared most about in the world? If this was to be his destiny, what kind of danger did that put Kelly in? He didn't know the answers, and he wasn't sure he wanted to know.

Kelly watched him go, a frown furrowing her brow. Hallucinations. Dalton had hallucinations. He'd also said he'd been up working all night. Surely that could account for the strange visions . . . the mirages of the mind.

Still, there was something about the whole thing that worried her. Something that nagged at the base of her brain, begging to be remembered, but refusing to develop.

She sat back down on the love seat, her thoughts on the man who'd just stumbled out of the room and upstairs. He'd looked dreadful, his eyes reflecting whatever horror the day of illusions had shown him. Why hadn't he told her exactly what he'd experienced? Had the hallucinations been too terrible to discuss? The shudder that had jolted his body had spoken more eloquently than any description he could have given.

Kelly's frown deepened as she suddenly thought of what it was that bedeviled her mind. Malcolm. He'd told them that Randolf had suffered horrible hallucinations. What was it he had said? That the hallucinations had been the beginning of the madness. *And Randolf had refused to discuss the specifics of his delusions, as well.*

Surely it was just his exhaustion, she told herself firmly. But this thought didn't stop the uncertainty that exhaled its chilling breath deep in her heart.

"Come shopping with me," Susan encouraged. "We haven't spent any time together at all since I moved in." Susan flopped down at Kelly's table, raising her furry slippers onto the chair opposite hers. "We can hit some of the boutiques, then get some lunch. It'll be like old times."

"Okay," Kelly agreed, thinking that perhaps a shopping trip with Susan would perk her up. For the past two days she'd once again felt that a gray pall had settled over the house. She'd seen very little of Dalton, who seemed to be consciously avoiding her. "Besides, the wallpaper store called me yesterday and told me my order was in. I can pick that up while we're out."

"Terrific." Susan's slippers hit the floor and she stood up. "I'll go shower and dress and we'll meet back here in about half an hour."

Kelly nodded, watching as her friend went out the door. Minutes later, standing in the shower, she tried to pinpoint the reason for the troubled disquiet she'd felt for the past couple of days.

She wondered if it wasn't just the fact that she was unsettled about Dalton, disappointed that he was keeping his distance from her. Despite his restraint, there were times in the night when she swore she knew he was thinking about her, times when she felt his energy drifting down the stairs and into her room, beckoning to her.

She'd fought against the mesmerizing potency of his silent call, knowing that if he wanted her with him, he'd come for her physically as well as *meta*physically. She was also still concerned about the hallucinations he'd confessed he'd suffered. Despite the fact that she had tried to convince herself it had merely been a weird manifestation of his overtiredness, it worried her.

Standing beneath the hot spray, she allowed her thoughts of Dalton to follow the water down the drain. She was spending too much time thinking about the man, obsessing about him. She was getting far too dangerously close to falling in love with him.

By the time she'd dressed and put on her makeup, Susan had returned, eager to begin their day of shopping and fun.

"You never told me if you'd sublet your apartment," Kelly observed as they drove away from the house and toward the small coastal town of North-hampton.

"Not yet. The woman I met the other day didn't like it. She said my furnishings weren't up to her standards." Kelly grinned at the indignation in Susan's voice. "I told her *she* wasn't up to *my* standards."

Kelly laughed, certain that her friend had done just that. She was suddenly very glad she'd decided to spend the day with Susan. Susan had always had a way of putting things into perspective, making worries seem minute.

Northhampton was an old town with a main street that was filled with funky and elegant boutiques, specialty stores for people with money to burn, and restaurants boasting famous chefs. At one time it had been a mecca for the beautiful people. Artists, actors, writers and the like had flocked to the area to build huge ocean-side escapes they could visit on the weekends and for summer vacations.

In the sixties and seventies, the area was abandoned by the wealthy, who had discovered new playgrounds, like the snow-covered slopes of Colorado and the hot, dry air of Arizona.

Recent years had brought a boom to the area as young professionals moved in, refurbishing the old homes and shops, renewing the glossy veneer the area had once possessed.

Kelly and Susan spent the morning trying on clothes in the little boutiques, laughing at new styles, reminiscing about the fads that had been popular when they'd been roommates in college.

"I wish we'd been around for bell-bottoms," Susan lamented as they walked down the sidewalk in search of a restaurant.

"I read someplace that they're making a comeback," Kelly observed, laughing as Susan grinned in delight.

"Wonderful. I always liked them because they make your calves and ankles look fat, which make thighs look thin, and my thighs can use all the help they can get."

"If you're worried about your thighs, then I assume you'll be ordering a salad for lunch?"

Susan looked at her in disbelief. "What, are you crazy? I plan on ordering the most fattening thing on the menu, then finishing up with a piece of cheesecake or something equally as decadent."

Kelly laughed and linked her arm with her friend's. "That's what I like about you, Susan. Your complete lack of willpower and discipline."

"So are you all set for the housewarming party?" Susan asked.

Kelly nodded. "I mailed out about twenty-five invitations two days ago."

"It should be loads of fun," Susan replied. "I'm definitely in the mood for a party."

"And I'm definitely in the mood for lunch!" Kelly exclaimed.

They passed several restaurants, finally settling on one that looked like an original landmark. The exterior was wood weathered to the color of pale sand. An ornate sign proclaimed the establishment to be the Beachcomber's Paradise.

Inside, Kelly and Susan were both delighted with the seafaring decor. Large fishing nets hung from the ceiling, studded with plastic crabs, starfish and sea horses. The booths were the color of the ocean, and the walls held photos of visiting celebrities who'd eaten here.

"Oh, look, here's the Marx Brothers," Susan exclaimed, pointing to a picture on the wall as they passed one of the tables. "I used to love their movies."

"Let's sit here," Kelly said, sliding into a booth and gesturing toward the picture of Randolf and Daphne that hung above.

Kelly looked at the picture of the two people who had owned her home. As always, she found herself captivated by Randolf's attractiveness and haunted by Daphne's ethereal beauty. In this photo, Daphne looked particularly beautiful and somehow heart-breakingly vulnerable. The slenderness of her face emphasized her wide eyes and lush full lips. Her face was one of contradictions, containing both the whisper of wild sexuality and a childlike quality. Her platinum-colored hair added to the dichotomy of innocence and abandonment.

Susan stared at the picture, too, a frown creasing her forehead. "I can't believe how much Dalton looks like his grandfather now that he's grown that mustache."

"He does, doesn't he?" Kelly agreed.

Susan hesitated a moment, then leaned over the top of the table. "There's something spooky about that man. He gives me the willies."

"Why?" Kelly looked at her friend in surprise. She'd never seen any indication of Susan's unease in Dalton's presence.

"I don't know." Susan leaned back against the blue leather of the booth, twisting a curl of her hair thoughtfully. "I've tried to put my finger on exactly what it is, but I can't . . . not really."

"Has he done something to you? Said something that makes you feel that way?" Kelly leaned forward.

"No, not to me specifically. I just think he's much too involved in the events of the past, the deaths of his grandparents. It's unhealthy, it's . . . weird." Susan released her strand of hair and wrapped her arms around herself as if she suffered from a sudden chill. "Like this morning . . . I got up early and when I came out of the apartment, Dalton was standing on the landing, staring down to the bottom of the stairs." Susan shivered and tightened her arms around herself. "I called out to him, but it was as if he didn't hear me. He just stared. I called to him again and he finally looked at me, but his eyes were so black and the look in them was so hateful. He looked just like I've always imagined Randolf looked when he was in the full throes of insanity."

Kelly was silent for a long moment. She remembered the night she had given Dalton the massage, when she'd awakened him. For a moment his eyes had been filled with such rage, such terrifying torment.

And then there was that fleeting image of him framed in the window, when he'd looked so crazy. And the hallucinations.... "Maybe he was just absorbed with his thoughts and resented the interruption," she finally suggested lamely.

"Maybe," Susan finally agreed reluctantly. "But I still say it's weird for him to be so obsessed with Randolf and Daphne's deaths. It's unhealthy, unnatural."

The conversation halted as the waitress approached to take their orders. When she had left, Susan leaned forward once again, her eyes dark with concern. "I think you should ask Dalton to leave, get him to move out of that house."

"What? I can't do that," Kelly protested. "And I *wouldn't* do that. I think you're overreacting to the whole situation. We probably spooked you that night we all sat around and talked about spirits and unhappy ghosts."

"I'm spooked, all right, but it's not by any ghosts or goblins." Susan sighed in frustration. She picked up her fork and pinged it against her water glass, then looked back at Kelly. "And I'm most worried about you getting involved with Dalton."

"Wha-what do you mean?" Kelly asked, feeling a warm blush rise to her cheeks.

"Come on, Kelly, don't try to tell me you don't feel something for him. Whenever the two of you are in a room together the air positively snaps and crackles between you." Susan reached across the table and touched Kelly's hand. "I'm just worried about you.

I've got bad vibes about him. I think he has the capacity to be dangerous.''

"I didn't know you got vibes," Kelly teased uneasily, trying to lighten the mood.

"Normally I don't. But something about Dalton definitely sends off little warning signals in my head. And the thing that concerns me is that you never get your vibes about yourself. Remember when I had that killer flu and thought I was going to die and you called because you'd been getting sensations that something wasn't right about me? Yet you had no warning whatsoever when you had that car accident." Again Susan's hand sought Kelly's and squeezed tightly. "Please take my word for it—something about Dalton isn't right. Promise me you'll stay away from him. Promise me you won't get involved with him on any level."

Kelly shook her head helplessly. She felt Susan's fear, knew it was genuine—it fairly radiated from her eyes—but she couldn't promise to stay away from Dalton. His lure was too powerful, the attraction too intense for her to deny or ignore. She knew her weaknesses, and she had a feeling that Dalton Waverly would prove to be her strongest one.

"I'll do my best," Kelly finally answered vaguely. But she feared it was already too late. She was already involved with Dalton, and nothing could change what had been put in motion. She thought again of those blank moments when he seemed so removed from reality. Was he merely a man intensely involved with his work, or was he a man on the verge of insanity?

They arrived at the house near dusk, laden with packages from their day of shopping. They parted ways on the stairs, each going to her own apartment.

Kelly kicked off her shoes and flopped down on the bed, her shopping bags beside her. Out of the first large sack she pulled a roll of the wallpaper she'd gotten for the living room. She studied the delicate floral print, pleased as she imagined it adorning the impressive walls.

While they'd been drifting in and out of the shops, she'd spied a purple velvet sofa reminiscent in style and color of the one that had once graced the room. She'd been unable to resist the temptation and had bought it, arranging a delivery date in ten days' time. That would give her enough time to finish the wallpapering.

She placed the bag of wallpaper rolls on the floor next to the bed, then opened the other sack. With a sigh of pleasure she withdrew the peignoir set. She'd found it in a thrift store and had instantly coveted it.

The gown was antique ivory silk, embroidered with tiny seed pearls. The robe was the same material, edged with fine lace. She'd once seen a picture of Daphne Weathers wearing a similar outfit. It had been accompanied by one of those "at home with the stars" interviews.

Unable to resist, Kelly quickly undressed and slipped it on. It hugged her to the waist, then flared into diaphanous folds that fell to the floor. She whirled around, allowing the skirt to billow like a cloud surrounding her. The movie stars of yesteryear knew how to dress to feel elegant and glamorous, she thought, watching her reflection in the dresser mirror.

She jumped as a knock resounded. Grabbing the robe, she pulled it on and opened the door to see Dalton.

The shadows of dusk that decorated the hallway clung to the hollows of his cheeks and emphasized the glittering depths of his eyes. As always at the sight of him, she found her breaths coming a bit more rapidly. "Hi," she said, feeling a blush of pleasure warming her cheeks.

"I came down earlier to see you, but you weren't here," he said.

"I went shopping." She tilted her head, studying him, recognizing instantly that, more than usual, he seemed to be a simmering cauldron of intensity.

"I'm finally getting around to viewing some of Randolf's old reels. I wondered if you'd like to come up and watch with me."

Kelly hesitated, Susan's recent warnings reverberating through her head. But the flashing danger lights faded beneath the glow of his eyes, the overt invitation that pulled her toward him, making Susan's fears seem silly and unfounded.

"I . . . I need to change clothes," she murmured.

"I'll wait for you."

"Give me ten minutes."

The moment she closed the door, shutting out his magnetic presence, hesitation once again set in. She couldn't ignore the fact that there was something about him that unsettled her. Maybe Susan was right. Maybe she really was a fool to get any more deeply involved with him. Perhaps the best thing to do was try to distance herself from him, forget him.

As she changed back into her jeans and blouse, she realized forgetting Dalton was an impossible option. The memory of his haunting touch, his exotic caresses, his demanding kisses, were burned forever into her mind and marked her soul.

Just as a spider's web captured and held its victims helpless, Dalton held a lure she was helpless to fight against. And worse than that, despite the tinge of danger she sensed from him, in spite of the fact that she recognized a dark force emanating from him, she wanted to be with him again.

CHAPTER NINE

A crazy feeling of dread mingled with a wild anticipation as she climbed the stairs to his room. The house was silent around her as if it, too, held its breath in expectation.

He opened the door before she could knock, as if he'd sensed her presence there. He didn't say a word. He took her hand and led her inside, where the film projector was set up on the table to display its celluloid images on the white screen across the room. A chair sat on either side of the table, also facing the screen. Dalton gestured for her to sit, then shut off the overhead light, plunging the room into complete darkness.

Kelly sat still, surrounded by the impenetrable blackness, waiting for Dalton to say something, waiting for the flick of a switch to begin the movie. She jumped in surprise as a hand touched her shoulder, then softly stroked the length of her hair.

"I'll keep the bathroom light on so I can see how to turn on the projector." Dalton's voice drifted to her from across the room, as the bathroom light flickered on.

Kelly stared at him in the semidarkness. If he was over there by the bathroom, then who had touched her shoulder? Who had caressed her hair? She whirled around, staring at the emptiness behind her.

I must have imagined it, she told herself as Dalton crossed the room and sat down in the chair on the other side of the table. It had been so soft, almost imperceptible. It had to have been her imagination. Still, she couldn't shake the cold fingers of apprehension that danced a waltz up her spine.

Dalton turned on the machine, the hauntingly familiar whir sending another set of fingers up her back. "What movie are we going to see?" she asked, trying to dispel the unsettling aura that permeated the room, the cold chills that still raced in an unsteady rhythm up her back.

"*The Forgotten Man.*" Dalton replied, his fingers working deftly to thread the film. "It was Randolf's last picture...shot fourteen months before his death."

The opening credits rolled, and Kelly settled back against the hard wood of the chair. Within minutes, she was completely engrossed in the film, marveling at the genius of the actor whose face was achingly attractive, his eyes unforgettably haunting, the resemblance to his grandson phenomenal.

As the story played out, she forgot about the eerie sensations she'd experienced moments earlier, forgot about the peculiar bond that existed between herself and Dalton.

She was completely captive to Randolf's magic, his ability to pull a viewer into his world, make them a part of the illusions he created within the movie. The same simmering intensity she'd felt from the moment she'd met Dalton, emanated from the wall where Randolf's face played bigger than life.

Kelly didn't know how long she'd sat, totally transfixed, when she realized there was a thin, ribbonlike smoky substance coiling around the screen. She watched in fascination as it curled and danced in a three-dimensional effect, appearing to extend out from Randolf's likeness. The temperature of the air surrounding her dropped dramatically, causing sudden goose bumps to rise up on her arms.

She watched in hypnotic fascination as the pale, foglike form gained substance and reached with tendril fingers toward Dalton.

It seemed to embrace him, wrapping around him like a shroud of mist. He didn't appear to be aware of it. His gaze was fixed on the screen, his eyes wide and staring. Faster and faster the mantle of mist spun around him.

As Kelly continued to stare in fascinated horror, the mist appeared to dissipate, although not in midair, but rather by invading him, seeping into his pores. As the last of the smoky substance disappeared, he slumped down in his chair.

The film reached its end, and the noisy clicking of the reel spinning round and round broke Kelly's inertia. She jumped up, the abrupt motion sending her chair crashing backward to the floor. The resulting noise didn't stir Dalton, who remained hunched over like a dead man.

She ran to the doorway and turned on the overhead light, then raced back to him. The air was warm again, as if the cold burst of arctic winds had only been her imagination. But Kelly knew it wasn't just a trick of her mind. The cold air had been real, just like the misty, foglike substance had been real. And yet there was a part of her that felt as if nothing was real...that since the moment Dalton had blown into this house, she'd been drifting in limbo in a place where fantasy and reality commingled, making it impossible to detect the difference.

However, reality was Dalton slouched over in the chair. Reality was the fear that squeezed the pit of Kelly's stomach, making her afraid she might be ill.

"Dalton?" She touched him gently on the shoulder, her fear growing, expanding inside her like an alien entity. She remembered the last time she'd awakened him, the look in his eyes in that unguarded moment when his gaze had been filled with such rage.

She was afraid of what his gaze would hold now, but was equally fearful of leaving him like this, somehow vulnerable in his unnatural sleep.

"Dalton?" She shook his shoulder more firmly, instantly releasing him and stepping away as his eyes flickered open.

He scrubbed his hands across his face, as if awakening from a deep, black sleep. "Kelly?" He looked at her in confusion.

"Dalton, what happened?" she asked.

He frowned and rubbed a hand across his forehead. "I must have fallen asleep. The movie's over," he observed, reaching over to turn off the clicking projector.

"Yes," she murmured, backing up toward the door. She felt a sudden, inexplicable need to be out of this room, away from him. She sensed something was wrong…frighteningly wrong. "I'm tired, too. I think I'll just head back down to my room." She didn't give him an opportunity to say anything.

She slipped out of his room and stumbled down the stairs, fighting off wave after wave of fear. It wasn't until she was safely locked in her room for the night that she allowed herself to think about what she'd experienced moments before.

She tugged off her jeans and blouse, her thoughts whirling frantically, trying to find a reasonable explanation for what she had seen. That threadlike mist had swirled around Dalton with obvious intent, as if it was a thinking, rational entity with drive and purpose.

"No," she protested. No, it had been smoke. Yes, that made perfect sense. The film projector had gotten hot and smoky and that was what she had seen.

Shivering, she pulled the long silk nightgown on over her head, finding the material uncomfortably cool. She added the lace-edged robe, then stretched out on the chaise lounge, her mind still racing with questions.

She could no longer deny that something was happening in this house, something that surrounded Dalton. Was it coming from him, or did it somehow threaten him?

"But what is it?" she whispered aloud, leaning her head against the chaise lounge.

Like a whispering at the edge of consciousness, like the flash of an image in one's peripheral vision, the strange energy she felt was nothing definite yet left a distinct impression.

Maybe Dalton *was* a man on the edge of sanity. What did she know about him really? Nothing except that he exerted some sort of bewitching spell on her that she was unable to resist. Was he slowly being pulled into the same sort of mental illness that had consumed his grandfather? Was that what she sensed in the air? Dalton's madness?

She jumped as she heard a light tapping on her door.

"Who is it?" she called, pulling her robe more closely around her and silently moving closer to the door. But she knew who it was and once again she felt an inexplicable fear licking at her insides.

"Let me in." Dalton's voice was a mere whisper, but it reverberated in her head like a vibrant demand.

"It's late, Dalton. I'm tired." As she remembered that strange smoke that had invaded his body, renewed anxiety coursed through her.

"I need you." The words filtered through the door, hypnotically soft, and she felt an evocative pull, enticing her to open the door, allow him entry. Still, she fought against it, her fear battling with her longing.

Something wasn't right, and until she had time to sort it out, think it through, she didn't want to let him in. She didn't think very well when he was near her.

She placed the palms of her hands on the wood of the door, able to feel his presence on the other side.

"I'll see you in the morning," she said, willing him to go before she lost her willpower and invited him in.

For a long moment she was aware that he remained on the other side of the door. She felt him silently beckoning her, summoning her to allow him entry. Then she felt nothing and knew he was gone.

She expelled a shaky breath and went back to the chaise lounge. She stretched out and shivered, exhausted by her mental turmoil.

She wanted him. Even now, her body yearned for his, ached with the need she knew he could sate. She wanted him as she'd never wanted a man, with an all-consuming demand that was impossible to ignore. But she was so afraid, afraid of things she couldn't comprehend.

There was no question, Dalton was losing his touch with reality. Those moments when he blanked out, stared into space...what was happening in his mind in those moments? That fleeting memory of him standing in the window, looking like a wild man.... Was he falling into the same pit of insanity that his grandfather had fallen into and never crawled out of, or was it something even more insidious than madness?

She sat up suddenly, aware of a noise, a whispering of movement within the wall of her room. It was louder than the scurry of mice, yet softly furtive. The hair on Kelly's arms prickled and stood at attention as her heart throbbed in unsteady rhythm.

Her eyes followed the sound, seeking its source. As she focused on the wall behind the narrow built-in bookcase, she suddenly realized what was making the noise, and her heart took up a new beat, one that was frenzied with wild anticipation. He was coming to her. He was coming to take her. She watched as the bookcase swung away from the wall, exposing the doorway to the secret passage that led to the attic rooms. And suddenly Dalton was there, filling the small space, his eyes black as the devil's and glittering with wildness.

In three long strides he crossed the room. He stood at the edge of the chaise, looming above her, his gaze holding hers, stealing her will to protest or deny the wild energy that pulsated between them.

His dark gaze swallowed her up, left her weak and wanting, consumed her in its very blackness, and she felt the room spinning, fading from reality as she fell into the darkness that beckoned her.

"Don't ever lock me out again," he whispered, his breath fanning her face with passion's heat. "We belong together without locked doors between us." He reached out and trailed a finger down the side of her face, then across the fullness of her bottom lip.

His caress lit a flame of white heat deep within her and she opened her mouth slightly and touched his finger with the tip of her tongue. He hissed his pleasure, his eyes blazing with a fire she knew would burn her soul forever.

Kelly knew at that moment that she was lost. It didn't matter to her if he was completely mad or not; she wanted him with a passion that transcended sanity itself. If he was crazy, so was she.

He leaned down and captured her lips with his, but it wasn't a mere kiss. It was a possession, as if he sought to steal the essence of her soul through the erotic potency of the kiss.

He didn't have to steal her soul—she willingly gave it, losing herself in a world of darkness where he was the only beacon of light, the only point of reality.

She started to rise, intent on leading him to the bed, but he stopped her, pushing her back against the chaise. "No...here," he whispered. "I want you right here." His hand stroked the satin textured material of the chaise, then moved to caress across her robe, pausing as his hand filled with the swell of her breast.

The glittering of his eyes intensified. "I want you here, naked against the satin." Kelly caught her breath at his deep, erotically sensual words. "Undress for me," he urged. He straightened, his eyes commanding her to do his bidding.

Her hands trembled as they moved to the belt of the robe. She was eager to comply, impatient to submit to the authority of his voice, the demand in his eyes.

She removed the robe, allowing it to fall in a silken puddle on the floor. The spaghetti straps of the nightgown fell down her shoulders, exposing her full breasts to the heat of his gaze. She paused as he unbuttoned his shirt and shrugged it off, exposing his broad shoulders and chest to her hungry eyes.

As she watched, he unsnapped his jeans and stepped out of them, his desire evident as he stood proudly, almost arrogantly, before her.

His hands rubbed up his lean outer thighs, then up to stroke across his broad expanse of chest. A small smile lifted one corner of his mouth, as if he found the feel of his own flesh surprisingly pleasing. It was the singularly most erotic action Kelly had ever seen, and as she felt his gaze lingering on her breasts, she felt her nipples responding, growing taut with a lustful desire she'd never felt before.

"Please..." she whispered, her need beyond reason, her craving beyond endurance. She removed the gown, wanting to be naked for him, needing him to take her now, on the cool satin chaise lounge.

"Please what?" he asked, his voice husky.

"Please love me." She opened her arms to him.

"Love you?" He lowered himself onto the lounge next to her, his flesh burning hers where it made intimate contact. He captured her face between his hands, peering deep into her eyes. "I do love you. My love is as timeless as forever, as lasting as infinity." And in the black abyss of his eyes, Kelly forgot the past, ignored the possibility of a future. She existed only in the present, in the reflection of his gaze.

With a devouring hunger he plundered her mouth with his, using his tongue as a weapon, as if to punish her with pleasure. As his lips claimed hers, his hands caressed first the fullness of her breasts, then the length of her body, finding all her secrets, lingering over her mysteries.

Where before when they had made love his touch had been gentle and tender, this time it was demanding and wild, spinning her into a world of sensation that was almost painful it was so exquisite. She lost all awareness of everything except the cool texture of the chaise against her back and the heat of his mouth and body against hers.

As his caresses grew more intimate, stroking boldly between her thighs, finding the core of her being, she cried out, clinging to him, spinning in a fiery vortex of passion that threatened to burn her alive. And then she was there, in the flames . . . igniting, burning, engulfed in fire, then rising out of the ashes to plead for more.

She clawed at his back, his shoulders, wanting him inside her, certain she would die if he didn't take her now. As he moved to hover above her, she arched, pressing into him, letting him know her intense need. He remained poised above her, his gaze holding hers, stroking inside her as intimately as his body touched hers. "You are mine," he whispered, and at the same moment he plunged into her.

"Yes," she hissed, tightening her legs around him, wanting to lock him inside her forever.

There was no finesse to their lovemaking, no civility. It was raw and harsh and frenzied. It was wild and lustful and powerful.

Kelly lost all sense of reality, all sense of self-identity. She was no longer Kelly and he was no longer Dalton. They were simply two entities spinning out of control together.

She was surrounded by darkness and knew only the sensation of him deep within her. She was vaguely aware of his deep groans and her own answering moans of desire. The sounds of their passion only fed her wildness.

She approached the edge of the fire pit once again, felt the deep, all-consuming heat beginning in her stomach and radiating outward. The feel of him stroking her so deep, invading her so completely, moved her closer and closer to the flames, and she cried out, hungry for the fire, yet afraid that once the flames licked at her soul she would be marked forever.

He seemed to sense her close proximity and increased the rhythm of their movements, encouraging her to dive into the fire, lose herself in their blazing heat.

She felt his body growing taut and knew he was losing control. She clung to him and together they dove off the cliff and into the fire, and in that single moment of complete unity, Kelly saw his soul, felt it wrap around hers. It was black and evil, and as it engulfed hers, she moaned in protest. Then there was nothing but the flames, burning her, swallowing her, and she was vaguely aware of Dalton's laughter surrounding her. She was conscious of lacy curtains billowing at the window, a hint of lilac mingling with the heavier scent of bay rum. Then blackness.

She shuddered and opened her eyes as he eased himself away from her. He stood for a long moment by the side of the chaise, his gaze caressing her as intimately as his hands and lips had moments before.

She wanted to say something, needed to laugh and dispel the invading horror she felt. But the darkness of his gaze stole her nervous laughter; the thick energy that radiated from him took away her inane words. She watched as he leaned down and grabbed his clothes, then walked back to the bookcase on the wall. When he reached it, he turned and looked at her, his gaze seeking hers across the expanse of the room. "You're mine, Daphne. Forever." His gaze held her for a long moment, then he turned and disappeared into the passageway.

Kelly didn't move until the bookcase swung back into position and the sounds of his furtive movements behind the wall were gone. Then she expelled a deep, shuddering breath.

Her hands shook as she bent over and picked up her robe and wrapped it around her, needing what warmth it could offer her to ward off the chill that had suddenly taken possession of her body.

Possession. That's what he'd done to her. He'd possessed her completely—not just her body, but her soul as well. Already her body ached from their intense lovemaking, but more frightening than the kinks and muscle pains was the deep-seated knowledge that something was dreadfully wrong.

She'd made love with Dalton before, had felt the tenderness of his caresses, but there had been little tenderness in what had just transpired.

She remembered the last time they had made love, that moment when Dalton's soul had touched hers. His had been filled with a radiant light, pure and white.

Pulling the robe more closely around her, she tried to ward off another shiver as she thought of moments before, when she'd once again felt Dalton's soul . . . a blackness so deep, so dark it had frightened her.

The shiver she'd tried to hold at bay swept over her, convulsively shaking her body with a tremble. *Daphne*. He'd called her Daphne. And he'd made love to her as if he was Randolf. It had been Dalton's lips that had kissed her, Dalton's hands that had caressed her, but it hadn't been Dalton who had made love to her. It had been a crazy man, a man who had fallen over the edge. . . . *A man who believed he was his evil, murderous grandfather.*

CHAPTER TEN

The wind whipped at Kelly's hair, swirling it around
her head so that she knew it would take forever to un-
tangle it. It was another gray morning, and she'd hesitated before venturing outside, but then decided she
needed to be out, away from the ominous aura of the
house. She needed to think and she didn't seem to do
that very well within the confines of Randolf's house.

She walked briskly, pulling the collar of her cable-
knit sweater closer around her neck. It seemed as if
she'd been cold forever. She wondered if she would
ever be warm again.

Crazy. Dalton was crazy. The words had swirled
around and around in her head in dizzying repetition
all night long. Somehow, Dalton had come to believe
that he was Randolf and she was Daphne, and if that
wasn't crazy, she didn't know what was.

Still, her mind rebelled against the very thought.
Even if she settled on the conclusion that Dalton *was*
insane, there were unanswered mysteries that kept
everything murky. She'd known from the moment
she'd moved into the house that something wasn't
quite right. She'd had a vague feeling that the house
was alive, that something alien resided within the
walls. All the little things that had happened—the

electrical shorts, the drafts of cold air... those things had intrigued her but had never really frightened her. She hadn't been truly frightened until last night, when she'd realized the man who'd stroked her body, the man who'd possessed her so completely, had not been Dalton at all. Who—or *what*—had made love to her?

Insane. The very word itself coiled in her head like a snake about to strike, filling her with horrifying dread. Insane like Randolf. Randolf, who had killed Daphne.

She kicked at the sand, confused as she considered those moments when she'd thought she'd seen lacy curtains at the bedroom window, smelled the distinctive scent of lilacs and bay rum. She frowned. How could Dalton's madness spill over to her? Insanity wasn't contagious. What had happened last night that had made her see things that weren't there, smell scents as if they lingered from the distant past?

No, surely it was more than insanity that infected the house, affected Dalton. But what?

She knew now whose window had been adorned with lacy curtains, who had been partial to the sweet scent of lilacs. Daphne. And the man who had sneaked down the hidden passageway and into her room had been Randolf. It hadn't been Dalton in some twisted, insane role-playing. It had been Randolf who had made love to her. She'd seen Dalton's soul and it had been white, but Randolf's had been black with bitterness, corrupt with anger.

Sitting down on the sand, she pulled her knees up against her chest and wrapped her arms around them, staring out at the water. Somehow, someway, the barrier between past and present had become transparent, allowing images to pass easily back and forth. But one thing was certain—it had not been an image of Randolf last night. And Dalton was not crazy.

Possession. The word coursed through her head, making her inner chill intensify. She tightened her grip around her knees, wishing for the sun to make an appearance. Surely if the sun was shining brightly she wouldn't be thinking such crazy thoughts.

But was it really so crazy? She'd sensed something present in the house, something unnatural, and if what she'd felt was the presence of Randolf's spirit, was it so crazy that he would possess the body of his grandson?

She raised her hands and rubbed at her temples, scooting around on her bottom so she faced the house. No longer did it look welcoming; rather it had taken on the characteristics of the house in Jeffrey's painting. There was an aura of evil invading the structure, a black cloud that didn't hover above, but emanated from within.

Rubbing her temples again, she released a deep sigh. She needed to talk to somebody. She needed another perspective.

Susan. Surely Susan would be a voice of reason.

She stood up and screamed as a hand touched her shoulder.

Whirling around, she saw Malcolm. "Oh God, Malcolm, you scared me to death." She expelled a shuddery puff of breath.

"I'm sorry, my dear. I didn't mean to frighten you." The old man smiled contritely.

"What are you doing out here?" she asked curiously.

"I try to take a little walk every morning. Keeps the bones mobile." His eyebrows raised up like gray question marks. "What brings you out here on such a dismal morning?"

Kelly hesitated, her gaze going back to linger on the house. "I'm worried about Dalton," she finally said.

"Ah yes, I've been most worried about him myself."

"You have?" Kelly looked at him in surprise.

"Indeed." Malcolm indicated he'd like her to walk with him and they moved farther down the beach at a snail's pace. "This obsession Dalton has with the death of his grandparents—it's most unhealthy. He's consumed with it, and in the past several days I've seen a steady regression of his mental capabilities."

Kelly stopped walking and looked at the old man in confusion. "I'm not sure I understand what you mean."

"Put quite simply, my dear, I think Dalton is falling victim to the same psychological illness as Randolf. He's going quite mad."

"No." Kelly's protest was a mere whisper. "No, it's more than that." She wasn't sure what frightened her more—the possibility that Dalton was possessed, or the possibility that he was insane and somehow so was she.

"Don't forget, I saw it with Randolf. I watched the steady progression of his mental deterioration. I was privy to all the little nuances, the subtle signs that portended his plunge into complete derangement." Malcolm shook his head ruefully. "It's like history repeating itself all over again. I see it all happening once again with Dalton. It brings back such horrible memories."

Kelly placed her hand on Malcolm's arm. "I don't think it's madness at all." She gave a self-conscious little laugh. "God, you're going to think I'm the one who's totally insane...but I'm beginning to think Dalton is possessed." The word hung in the air for what seemed like an eternity.

Malcolm stared at her. "Possessed?" he finally repeated. There was a slight edge of amusement in his tone. "And what, or *who,* might I ask, do you think has possessed him?"

"It's Randolf. I've felt him, Malcolm." She started walking again, slowing her pace so he could keep up with her. "I know it sounds crazy, but I've felt his presence in the house since the moment I moved in. I've even smelled him. He used to wear bay rum, didn't he?" She exclaimed in triumph at Malcolm's expression. "He did! I smell it when Dalton is around. I've felt Randolf's spirit and I really think his spirit has taken possession of Dalton's body."

She frowned. Saying the words out loud, she suddenly realized how ludicrous they sounded. She wouldn't be surprised if Malcolm called in the men in white jackets to take her away for a long rest.

"If I believed what you're saying...and I don't...why on earth would Randolf want to possess Dalton?"

Kelly's frown deepened as she rolled the question over in her mind. Why indeed? "I don't know," she confessed. "Why is he still here? Why hasn't he moved on to wherever ghosts go? I don't know, Malcolm. I only know what I feel, and I refuse to believe that Dalton is crazy."

Malcolm stared at her for a few moments, then sighed, a sigh of weariness and age. "And Daphne refused to believe that Randolf was crazy, and you see where that got her." His words caused a wintry hand to clutch at Kelly's heart. "Kelly, my dear, I've seen the romantic sparks between you and Dalton. He looks at you the same way Randolf used to look at Daphne. As if he could consume you with his gaze alone." Malcolm stopped walking once again and turned to face her, his face a study of concern. "Be careful, Kelly. I fear for you. If Dalton is suffering from the same dementia as Randolf, then you might be in danger."

"That's ridiculous," Kelly scoffed uneasily. "Dalton could never harm me." But could Randolf? She rubbed at her temples, confusion creating a pounding headache.

"Just be careful," Malcolm replied, touching her arm lightly. "Dalton is following in the path of Randolf, and it was a path that led straight to hell, a path that resulted in Daphne's tragic death."

"I know," she whispered, then turned around. "I think I'll head back to the house."

"I'm ready to go in, too," Malcolm agreed. "I see our young artist friend is busy at work." He pointed ahead to where Jeffrey had made an appearance and was setting up his easel and paints.

"He's a nice kid," Kelly said. "And he's quite talented. He gave me one of his paintings the other day and I was quite impressed."

Jeffrey smiled in greeting as they approached him. "I think the sun's taken a permanent leave of absence," he said as they drew closer.

Even his shy, cheerful smile couldn't dispel the trepidation that Malcolm's words had evoked in Kelly. Still, she forced a smile to her lips. "Yes, it has been unusually gloomy for the last several weeks."

"Oh, I went to your room looking for you earlier. My kitchen sink isn't draining very well."

"I'm going on inside," Malcolm said, waving as he headed on toward the house.

Kelly watched him go, then turned back to Jeffrey. "I've got some liquid drain cleaner. Why don't we give that a try, and if that doesn't work I'll get a plumber out to look at it."

Jeffrey nodded. "Sounds good. You want to do it now?"

"Sure," Kelly agreed. "Are you at a place where you can stop and let me into your rooms?"

Jeffrey wiped off his paint brush on a rag. "Let's do it," he said, falling into step beside her.

"I'll be right with you. I'll just grab the cleaner," she said as they entered the house. She went into the kitchen and grabbed the bottle from the cabinet, then went to Jeffrey's room.

She hadn't been in his area since he'd moved in and she was surprised at how the place had taken on his personality. Scented candles of all shapes and sizes were scattered around the room, their lingering scent filling the air with fragrance.

The ceiling was covered with a white sheet, painted to depict sunlit, fluffy clouds. Another sheet hung on one wall, containing a rainbow with a unicorn dancing atop the colorful bands. And everywhere in the room, resting on the floor, set on top of the end tables, positioned in the corners, were paintings.

Where the room itself contained a sort of fanciful cheerfulness, the paintings were dark, disturbing, blending light fantasy and dark demons to create pictures that intrigued, yet were troubling at the same time.

"Jeffrey, these are magnificent," Kelly exclaimed, walking slowly around the room, trying to look at each and every masterpiece. She paused in front of another painting of the house, again struck by his blend of reality and fantasy.

In this particular painting, the house was veiled in shadows and there was a dark cloud spitting lightning hovering above. She leaned closer, particularly struck by his attention to detail. Strange, ghostlike entities seemed to be visible at each window, like prisoners trying to escape a jail.

"What a disturbing painting," she observed. She looked at Jeffrey curiously, wondering if he possessed some sort of psychic power that made him sensitive to the seething energies of the house.

"Ah, it's just imagination." He grinned sheepishly. "Knowing about that Randolf guy and the history of the house, it's easy to imagine everything dark and spooky with restless ghosts wandering around. Besides, my agent says this is the kind of thing that sells."

She looked at him in surprise. "You have an agent?"

He nodded proudly. "We're planning to have a showing in the next three months. He's found a gallery that's tentatively agreed to display my work."

"Oh, Jeffrey, that's wonderful news." Kelly gave him a quick, impulsive hug, smiling as a hot blush swept over his face and reddened the tips of his ears. "Now, I'd better get to that sink so you can get back to work."

She went over to the sink and quickly read the instructions on the side of the bottle of drain cleaner. "This is supposed to work for fifteen minutes, then be washed down with hot water." She poured half the bottle down the drain.

"Would you mind running the water?" Jeffrey asked hesitantly. "I'd sort of like to get back outside before it gets too late in the day. Even when there's no sun, the lighting is best in the mornings."

"Go on," Kelly told him with a smile. "I'll relock the door when I'm finished."

He flashed her a grateful smile, then disappeared out of the room.

When he had gone, Kelly walked back over to the painting of the house, staring at it thoughtfully. It was odd how it seemed to reflect Kelly's own perceptions. Something else odd was the fact that she still got no sensations of energy from Jeffrey. Even when she had hugged him, she'd felt nothing—no colorful hues, no radiating energy.

And now that she thought about it, it was the same with Malcolm. She felt nothing from him, either. There had been people before who she'd felt nothing from...no vibrations, no auras, no sense of soul. But they were rare.

Perhaps it had something to do with age. Maybe it was Jeffrey's youth and Malcolm's advanced years. She dismissed the oddity from her mind and moved back over to the sink. She had work to do, and then she had to think, think about what in the hell was happening in this house...and what was happening to Dalton.

Dalton stared out the window, his head throbbing with a nauseating intensity. "She's mine," he whispered, staring at the beach where Kelly had stood only moments before. He blinked rapidly, the headache making it hard to see, difficult to think.

She was his, but even now she was betraying him by sleeping with the young artist. Black anger filled him at the thought, and his heart rebelled. But he knew it was true. Only this morning his computer screen had told him of her faithlessness, and his brain had been filled with visions of her treachery.

He'd watched as the two of them had left the beach together, and he'd heard the sound of them disappearing into the artist's room.

He'd been easily able to imagine her soft, sweet body beneath the young man's eager caresses. His mind had saturated itself with erotic images of her moaning her pleasure as the artist ran his fingers down her body like paintbrushes on canvas. He would paint her body with his fingertips, with his lips, tasting all the sweetness that by rights belonged to another.

The visions tormented him, caused the sickening pounding in his head to intensify. It wasn't fair. *It just wasn't fair.* "She belongs to me," he said aloud.

He reeled away from the window, feeling the heat of his wrath rising up inside him, threatening an eruption of mammoth proportions. *Damn her.* Why was she doing this? Why was she betraying their passion, their love? She had no right to mock what they had between them. She had no right to do this to him.

Damn her. If she'd just be patient, things would get better again. The house would fill with laughter and friends, and their life would be golden once more.

If she'd just give him a chance to turn things around. He'd get another role. He frowned. Another role? Where had that thought come from? God, each day it grew more and more difficult to think... to concentrate. He rubbed at the center of his forehead, the pain once again so intense it nearly blinded him.

He turned and stumbled toward the bed. Perhaps if he rested for just a little while, the headache would go away. Then he could think...he could plan what must be done with her.

Kelly watched in satisfaction as the water drained smoothly. She gave the sink a final rinse, then turned off the faucet.

Leaving the bottle of drain cleaner on the counter in case Jeffrey should need it again, she turned and left his room, carefully locking the door behind her.

She gasped as a hand fell on her shoulder. Spinning around, she found herself looking into Dalton's black, angry gaze. "We need to talk," he said, grabbing her hand and pulling her up the stairs toward her room. His grip was hard, almost painful, and a black cloud of energy surrounded him, making Kelly's heart thud a harsh rhythm against her ribs.

As they reached the landing, Kelly wrenched her hand from his and faced him, Malcolm's warnings swirling around in her head. Crazy or possessed, she didn't know what was wrong with him, but she knew he was angry... angrier than she'd ever seen him before. And in his wrath she sensed danger, a danger far greater than any she had ever faced.

There was no way she was going to let him get her in her room alone, not while his anger was such a living, breathing force.

"We can talk here," she said smoothly. She grabbed on to the stair railing, feeling like she needed an anchor against the stormy sea of his eyes.

His gaze moved from her, down to the stairs, and remained for a long moment at the bottom. A chill of horror raced up Kelly's spine as she realized this must have been the very place where Daphne and Randolf had had their final moments together. Whatever had happened that had led to their deaths had happened at this very place. Kelly's hand tightened around the railing.

His eyes swept back to her, and for just a moment she saw confusion mingling with the rage. "Not here," he said hoarsely. Then the confusion was gone, leaving only his overwhelming fury to color his onyx eyes. "What I have to say to you is private."

He reached for her and she took a step backward, releasing her hold on the banister as her foot caught on the edge of the stairs.

Suddenly Kelly had the sensation of falling. Her hands flailed ineffectually at the air and she felt her body falling, thudding on the stairs, hitting painfully against the hard wood. And then she was once again standing at the top of the staircase, held tightly against the broad strength of Dalton's chest.

She gasped a sob, realizing that through some sort of strange phenomena, she'd just experienced Daphne's final descent down the stairs.

"We need to talk, but not here," he repeated, and this time she nodded her agreement, allowing him to lead her into her room. He seemed unaware of what had just happened, what she'd just experienced. He stood in the center of the room, as if gathering his thoughts.

She sat down on the edge of the bed, her legs too weak to hold her upright. It had felt so real. Not so much as if she was Kelly experiencing Daphne's death, but as if, for that single instant in time, she had actually *been* Daphne.

Was that how it had happened? Had Randolf and Daphne fought and she'd accidently fallen? Then why had Randolf gotten a gun and shot her? It didn't make sense. None of this made sense.

She looked up at Dalton, wondering why he didn't seem to realize what had just happened, that somehow the past had reached out and struck them both.

He paced the room with long strides, his muscles taut and rigid, his anger still rolling off him in waves. As she watched, he turned and glared at her. "You're sleeping with him."

It was a statement, not a question, and for a long moment Kelly looked at him in confusion, wondering what on earth he was talking about. "I'm *what?*"

"Don't play the innocent with me. It doesn't become you."

"I'm not playing anything. I don't know what you're talking about."

He raked his hand through his hair, causing it to stand on end, giving him a slightly demented aura. "I know. You can't deny it. I know what you're doing behind my back."

"Dalton . . . I really don't know what you're talking about," Kelly exclaimed. She stood up and walked toward him, her hands out in supplication. "Dalton . . . talk to me. What is it you think I'm doing behind your back?''

"Sleeping with that boy," he snarled, his wrath once again filling the room. "Tell me, does he please you like I do? Does he make you moan deep in your throat like you do with me?" He reached out and stroked her hair with a deceptive softness. "Why?" His voice was tortured. "I know things haven't been terrific lately, but why do this to me . . . to us?"

"Dalton . . ." She reached up and placed her hands on either side of his face, trying to see beneath the rage, looking for the goodness she knew was hidden beneath the anger. "I'm not sleeping with anyone but you. I'm not," she stressed, but she could see by his expression that he was beyond listening to her.

He moaned and grabbed a handful of her hair. "Don't lie to me. For God's sakes, I don't deserve your lies." His grip on her hair tightened, becoming almost painful. "Just tell me you'll never sleep with him again. We can get past this. . . . Just tell me you'll never see him again."

"You're hurting me," she breathed, gasping in relief as he released his hold on her hair. "I still don't understand. Who do you think I'm sleeping with?"

He spun away from her, his hands working in the air as if he was looking for something to break, something to hit. He turned around and stared at her. "The pool man," he finally bellowed, the force of his roar propelling her back several steps. He looked completely insane . . . his hair on end, his eyes wild and haunted.

"The pool man?" She eyed him in bewilderment.

Again, for just a single moment, confusion muddied his expression. "I mean the artist . . . the artist," he said wildly. "You know who I'm talking about. You know what you're doing." He paced the room again, stopping in front of her dresser, where the painting Jeffrey had given her rested against the mirror. He picked it up, his hand shaking with suppressed emotion. "I should kill him."

Kelly hissed a swift intake of breath at the vehemence of his words. He threw the painting against a wall, the force of the throw causing it to bounce twice before it finally fell to the floor. He then turned back and stared at her. *"Or I should kill you."*

She held her breath as he approached her, a bitter smile curving his lips upward. She couldn't move. Her fear froze her to immobility. "I should kill you," he whispered, his arms wrapping around her as he pulled her against his chest. "But I could never hurt you. . . . I love you." He whispered the words into her ear, then his lips moved in a heated blaze down the side of her neck. "Maybe the best thing for me to do is love you so completely, so thoroughly, that you'll never want anyone else but me." His kisses were hot and demanding against the hollow of her neck. "I'll kill you with love, make it impossible for you to ever love anyone else."

As his lips took hers, she became aware of the distinctive scent of bay rum. It had been present in the room for some time but she just now realized it. The tangy smell sent warning signals flashing in her head.

"Wait," she said frantically, pushing against his chest, trying to break his embrace. "Stop," she protested, her panic rising up to choke her.

"Don't deny me," he replied hoarsely. With an unnatural strength, he swept her up and carried her toward the chaise lounge. He put her down on the satin material and instantly covered her, his hands ripping at her blouse with a fevered intensity as his mouth sought to possess hers.

"Please don't...not like this," she said. Even though his mouth tasted like Dalton's and his hands were Dalton's hands, the entire situation frightened her. She wanted it to stop.

"Dalton, please don't do this... Please stop...." Her feverish protests were smothered beneath the demanding pressure of his lips against hers.

His mouth was like a hot wind, carrying her out to storm-tossed seas. Despite the fact that she knew it was wrong—*he* was all wrong—Dalton's lips plied hers with heat, causing her protests to seem like the vague, ineffectual beating of moth wings against a screen door. She struggled to maintain control, whimpering another flurry of objections. She felt as if she was drowning...drowning in the sensual semidarkness he wove around her.

He paused, his breath hot on her face, the scent of bay rum overwhelming. He looked down at her, his eyes the tormented eyes of a man in pain. "Please, don't deny me what you give so freely to the man who cleans the pool."

She stared at him, fighting against the waves of darkness his kisses evoked. The scent of bay rum was stronger than ever, and again she was afraid. "Dalton, there is no pool man." She placed her hands on either side of his face. "There is no pool." She said the words firmly, shoving against him with renewed strength. He reached for her once again, his hands hot with fevered need.

"For God's sakes, listen to me," she half sobbed. *"There...is...no...pool."*

In an instant a myriad of emotions reflected on his features. The rage left his eyes, the tautness of his muscles relaxed and the blackness that had surrounded him dissipated. Vulnerability replaced the rage, torture filled his eyes.

He flung himself up and off the chaise lounge, his hands clenched into fists and pressed against the side of his head. "Dear God, what's happening to me? Help me, Kelly," he whispered. "Dear God, please help me." With an agonized groan, he fled the room.

For a long moment after he'd gone, Kelly remained on the chaise lounge, too stunned to move. She knew now... knew with a certainty that couldn't be denied. Malcolm had been wrong. Dalton wasn't crazy. He was possessed, possessed with the spirit of Randolf.

She didn't know what Randolf wanted, why he had chosen to return to this plane of existence. He had Dalton, but not completely. Her heart cried out as she thought of that instant when the rage had left, and she'd seen the tortured gaze of Dalton without Randolf's influence.

She had to help him. She had to do something to save Dalton, gain back his soul, remove Randolf's presence. She had a feeling she was the only one in the world who could help him. But what? What? Why was Randolf here? What did he want from Dalton? From her?

She thought again about that moment on the stairs, when she had experienced Daphne's fall. It had been so vividly real.

Had Randolf truly killed his wife? Was he evil and insane? Had he taken possession of Dalton because he needed a physical body to continue his evil?

And if he was back and he thought she was Daphne, then what sort of mortal danger was she in? In trying to help Dalton was she putting her own life at risk?

CHAPTER ELEVEN

It was midmorning when Kelly finally got out of bed. She'd had a horrible night. She'd remained awake for a long time, listening to the house breathe. The subtle shifting noises, the creaking and groaning that she'd once found vaguely comforting, now filled her with unease. Were they the normal sounds of an old house, or were they something more ominous... the sounds of spirits trying to make contact? And if they were spirits, what did they want? Why were they here?

She'd finally drifted off to sleep only to suffer horrifying dreams. Dreams of falling, of seeing Dalton standing at the top of the stairs as she plummeted to the bottom. Dreams of gunshots and death and demonic laughter and possessive rages.

She dressed quickly, her thoughts filled with Dalton and the jealousy that had consumed him the day before, that single moment when the real Dalton had looked at her with tortured eyes and pleaded for her help.

But how could she help him? What could she do? This wasn't a movie and she couldn't call ghostbusters to exorcise him. She bent over and picked up Jeffrey's painting from the floor, where Dalton had flung it last night.

How had he ever gotten the crazy idea that she was sleeping with Jeffrey? Jeffrey wasn't anything more than a pleasant boy, a talented youth.

She tucked the painting safely away in a dresser drawer, frowning thoughtfully. And why had Dalton kept insisting she was cheating with the pool man? There was no pool here. None of it made any sense.

If she was going to help Dalton, she had a feeling that she needed to solve the mystery of Daphne and Randolf's deaths. She needed to know exactly what had happened that fatal night, if for no other reason than to ensure her own safety. If Randolf had taken possession of Dalton's body and thought she was Daphne, then she needed to know how to prevent the past from repeating itself. In learning exactly what had happened so many years ago, she might be able to help Dalton, but more important, she might just save her own life.

She left her room and immediately went up the narrow stairs to Dalton's, drawn there by a need to see him, a need to connect with him. She knocked on his door, hoping that he would answer and be Dalton... the real Dalton, without the black rage ringing his eyes, without the aura of threat surrounding him.

There was no answer. She knocked again, calling his name, but still there was no reply. She twisted his doorknob. The door was locked. She knew he was inside. She could feel him in there. She called his name one last time, then sighed in defeat. She'd check on him again later.

She went back downstairs, meeting Malcolm as he came out of the study. "You were just the person I was coming to see," she said.

"Indeed? Well, here I am."

"I was wondering if you could tell me if there was ever a swimming pool here?"

Malcolm's gray eyebrows danced up in surprise. "How did you know about that?"

She shrugged. "I don't know. I read something about it someplace or another." For some reason she didn't want to tell him she'd heard about it from Dalton. Malcolm didn't believe in ghosts, had made it clear he didn't believe that Dalton was possessed. She knew he wouldn't believe her if she told him she'd learned of the pool from the spirit that now inhabited Dalton's body.

"There was a pool initially, but Randolf had it filled in. It was one of the bizarre things he did when he was going over the edge. Why?"

"Just curious," Kelly answered. "Also, would you mind making out a complete guest list of all the people who were at the party the night Randolf and Daphne died?"

"What on earth for?" he asked in surprise.

Again Kelly shrugged. "I'm beginning to believe Dalton when he says that something happened that night, something other than the official version of their deaths."

Malcolm shook his head sadly. "And so now you've become infected with Dalton's obsession." He touched her arm, his forehead deeply wrinkled in concern.

"Can't you see that Dalton is ill? Who knows, perhaps the madness was genetic and Dalton would have gone over the edge no matter where he was or what he was doing. Or maybe in coming to this house and delving into the past, he called up the madness that had hidden inside him for so many years." His fingers squeezed on her arm. "You must understand, the sickness has caused him to take on the traits of his grandfather, and that puts you at enormous risk."

He released his hold on her and once again shook his head. "He'll never finish the book now. Let it rest, Kelly. The past has already harmed Dalton, don't let it suck you in as well."

Kelly thought of Dalton, the torment on his face in that single moment of vulnerability. "I can't let it rest," she finally answered. "I have to find out what exactly happened on the night Randolf and Daphne died."

"Then I fear for your life," he replied, his words blowing cold winds of uncertainty through her.

"But you'll make out a guest list of that night?" she pressed.

He hesitated a moment, then nodded. "Of course. I'll do whatever I can to help you."

Kelly nodded, watching as the old man turned and disappeared into his room. Thoughtfully she walked into the living room, where the new wallpaper rested in a stack in the corner, awaiting her labor to transform the room.

She set to work, knowing that she found it easiest to think clearly when she did physical activity. Her housewarming party was a scant two weeks away. The first of the RSVPs had come in the mail the day before. Perhaps I should cancel, she thought. But for some reason she knew she wouldn't.

The cards of fate had been sent tumbling, and she had a feeling the party was an important aspect of whatever fate had planned for all of them. She felt a storm approaching, one that had nothing to do with nature's elements, but rather a storm of energies converging, setting up a battleground of forces that terrified her. Yes, it terrified her, but she felt it was as inevitable as the sun setting that evening and rising again in the morning sky.

Again uncertainty swept over her. Was Dalton truly possessed or was he completely insane? Was Malcolm right? Was Randolf's insanity genetic, and the defective genes had merely been waiting like insidious cancer cells that attack the system unexpectedly? Was Dalton only manifesting traits that would make her assume he was possessed? Was that, indeed, only part of the madness?

What about the smells she'd experienced? He couldn't have caused that to happen through sheer lunacy. And he'd known about the pool. If he wasn't truly possessed, then how had he known that? A single note in an obscure newspaper article, a mention in a fan magazine? Dalton *could* have read about the pool, or heard about it from a number of sources. "Damn," she exclaimed, her inner confusion causing her to rip a piece of the wallpaper.

Had Randolf filled in the pool because he suspected Daphne of having an affair? *Had* she been having an affair? Had he killed her in a jealous rage? Her hands trembled as she smoothed a new piece of wallpaper into place.

Dalton's rage yesterday had been awesome, his jealousy unfounded but as real to him as the very house that surrounded him. Was it that same sort of rage that had resulted in Daphne's death?

She worked for the rest of the morning, questions swirling around her head in a haunting rhythm, questions that had no definitive answers.

At noon she decided to go talk to Susan. Maybe she could put a new perspective on things. She found her friend scrubbing out the oven, the window of the room open to air out the ammonia scent of the cleaner she used.

"How was I supposed to know potatoes would explode if you baked them and didn't poke them?" she grumbled, yanking off the rubber gloves and gesturing for Kelly to have a seat at the small dinette table. "So what's happening?"

Kelly recognized a slight edge of hysteria in her answering burst of laughter to the casual question. Oh, not much, she thought. I've got a crazy or possessed man living in my attic, I made love to a spirit the other night and I think there's a distinct possibility that he's going to try to kill me. She swallowed these words and shrugged her shoulders. "Not much, although I'm finding myself more and more intrigued by Daphne and Randolf's deaths."

Susan frowned. "How morbid." She dropped her gloves in the sink and joined Kelly at the table. "Why would you want to know any of the gory details of deaths that happened so long ago?"

Self-preservation, Kelly thought, but once again she bit back the words. She leaned forward and eyed Susan intently. "Susan, I think Randolf's ghost is haunting this house."

"If you're trying to scare me, you're doing a bang-up job," Susan replied uneasily.

"I'm not trying to frighten you." Kelly leaned back and sighed deeply. "Haven't you felt anything weird? Smelled unusual odors? Felt cold drafts that come from nowhere?"

"The only thing weird I've seen in this house is the man you've got staying upstairs," Susan countered. "And he's getting more and more weird with every day that passes."

"I think he's possessed," Kelly breathed, watching the play of emotions on her friend's face. A fleeting look of horror was quickly usurped by disbelief.

"I think *he's* possessed *you,*" she retorted. "Kelly, make him leave. Kick him out of here. He scares me. I think he's some kind of a psychopath. Did you know he stopped Gary in the hall yesterday and told him to stay away from you?"

Kelly looked at her in surprise. "He did?"

Susan nodded. "Gary said he looked exactly like Randolf. He had his hair all slicked back and he looked like he'd stepped out of an old movie. It freaked Gary out completely."

"But don't you see? He looked just like Randolf because he *was* Randolf. Randolf has taken him, body and soul, and I can't help Dalton unless I figure out why Randolf is here, what he wants."

"You love him." Susan stared at her incredulously. "That's why you've come up with this crazy scenario. You love him, and it's easier to think he's possessed by some wicked spirit than to believe the man is insane."

"That's ridiculous," Kelly scoffed with a frown, a headache blossoming in the center of her forehead. But was it so ridiculous? Was her mind playing tricks on her, trying to rationalize Dalton's strangeness because she cared about him? Had she smelled the strange scents associated with Daphne and Randolf or had she merely imagined the scents, playing into Dalton's derangement? "I'm not sure what I feel for Dalton.... All I know is that Dalton's spirit is pure and good, and the spirit I sense in him now isn't. It's filled with a rage I don't understand."

"Okay." Susan folded her hands on top of the table. "Let's just say for argument's sake that Randolf *has* possessed Dalton. Why hasn't he moved on? Why is he still hanging around here, taking over people's bodies?"

"I don't know," Kelly said in defeat.

"From everything I've read, it's believed that ghosts generally return to this plane if they've suffered sudden, violent deaths and don't realize they've died. But that can't be the reason for Randolf's return—Randolf killed himself. Even on the astral plane he'd know he was dead."

"But there are other reasons why ghosts return to this plane," Kelly protested. "Like being attached to a specific person or place and being unable to release themselves to go on and leave these things behind."

"But according to everything we know, Randolf's one big obsession was with Daphne, and she's dead, too. There's no reason for him to hang around here. They're together."

"Then, revenge," Kelly replied. "Maybe he's come back for revenge."

"Revenge for what?" Susan expelled a frustrated sigh. "I'll tell you what I think—if Randolf is truly a spirit and haunting this place, it's because he was a wicked, evil man and now he's a wicked, evil spirit looking for a body to take over so he can continue his malevolence."

Susan leaned forward and grabbed Kelly's hand. "Don't you see, Kelly. No matter what is happening, you're in danger. Dalton is obsessed with you, and if he's crazy, who knows what form that obsession might take. And if he's possessed, then it's a vile evilness that has possessed him and we're all in danger."

"But no matter what's happening, he needs me. He needs my help," Kelly protested.

"Dammit, Kelly." Susan slapped her hands down on the table. "If the man is crazy, then he needs professional help, and if he's possessed, then you're delving into areas that are dangerous not just to your life, but to your very soul." She scooted her chair away from the table and stood up. "Tell him to leave, Kelly. Get him out of this house before something terrible happens. This isn't a children's game—this is something worse than a Ouija board. This is evil and you're in it too deep."

Kelly nodded and stood as well. "You're right," she agreed. "I'm in too deep, and that's exactly why I *can't* get out. I can't ask him to leave. It's gone too far. It has to play out."

Susan looked at her for a long moment, her blue eyes darkened with fear. "I'm afraid for you."

Kelly nodded, hesitating. "I'm afraid, too," she finally answered truthfully. With this, she turned and left.

She walked down the stairs and hesitated at the foot, trying to pick up sensations from this place of long-ago death. But there was nothing. Still, she couldn't shake the feeling that the mystery of what had happened between Daphne and Randolf on that last night held the key to all the events that were unfolding now.

She frowned, a flash of movement in the corner of her eye pulling her thoughts away from the past. Malcolm had just gone into the study. Curious, she headed in that direction, wondering if he was looking for her.

She entered the study, surprised to find it empty. But she knew she'd seen somebody come in...and for some reason, she'd thought it was the old man. She shrugged, realizing she must have just imagined it. Unless the old man had the ability to disappear into thin air, it had to have been her imagination.

For the rest of the afternoon Kelly wallpapered, her mind no clearer than it had been that morning. It felt odd, sublimely ridiculous, doing something so mundane as transforming walls while around her swirled mysteries of supernatural proportions. Yet she didn't know what else to do.

It was nearing dusk when she smelled the now-familiar odor of bay rum. Turning around, she saw Dalton standing in the doorway, a small, enigmatic smile curving his sensual lips. His hair was slicked back, exposing fully the haunting shadows of the hollows and planes of his face.

"You look lovely with the twilight sweeping in through the windows," he said, stepping into the room and over to where she stood.

"Thank you," she replied, unsure how to react to him, afraid that a single wrong word might arouse his anger. She set aside her brush and rubbed her hands nervously down the side of her jeans.

"The new paper looks good," he observed, reaching to draw her into his embrace.

"I should have it all finished before the party next week." She fought the impulse to melt against him, the scent of bay rum still strong within the room. She wanted Dalton's arms around her, wanted to feel the steady rhythm of his heart beating against her own. But she knew it wasn't Dalton's arms enfolding her, it wasn't his soul she saw in those dark eyes.

"The party will be good," he said, his hands moving slowly, sensually down her back, as if he was memorizing each curve, every line. He pulled back from her and gazed at her intently. "It will truly be a night to remember." He smiled again, only this time the smile held a haunting quality that made a shiver dance up her spine.

"Come upstairs with me," he urged suddenly, pulling her back against the length of his body. "I'm tired of working for today. I want you." His hands grew more bold, cupping her buttocks and drawing her into him, letting her know the extent of his arousal.

The feel of him so hard, so fully extended against her, filled her with a further horror. Although she knew it was Dalton's body she felt, her emotions raged in protest. It felt like betrayal. She couldn't make love to him. She wanted Dalton, and she knew with a gut-wrenching certainty it wasn't he who would make love to her.

"I've still got so much work to finish up in here," she protested lightly, sliding out of his embrace and once again picking up her wallpaper brush. "Maybe later," she hedged.

He stared at her, his eyes dark, glittering. What was it Malcolm had said? Something about a gaze that consumed. . . . Yes, that was how she felt, completely consumed by his gaze. "You'll come to me tonight?"

Although she wanted to deny it, she couldn't. There was something inside her that couldn't resist the burning obsession in his eyes, couldn't withstand the assault on her senses. "Yes," she whispered, feeling as if the reply came from a dark place inside her, a place where she wasn't in control.

"Then I'll wait for you tonight, and you'll come to me when the whole house sleeps." He smiled again, that slightly twisted gesture that once again sent a shiver through Kelly's soul. "And I'll make you forget all the others. I swear I'll make you truly mine forever."

He turned and left, and the room once again smelled of wallpaper paste and the crisp fall breeze blowing off the ocean and in through the window.

Kelly sagged against the wall, as always feeling like he'd taken all the energy out of the room, out of *her* when he left. She shook her head, wondering what had possessed her to agree to go to him. Of course she wouldn't. She couldn't. He wasn't Dalton, and she wasn't the woman Randolf wanted. Unfortunately, he didn't seem to be aware that she wasn't the woman he loved. She hoped he realized she wasn't Daphne before the past played out in its entirety. She definitely didn't want to meet the same violent, tragic end as the woman Randolf had loved.

Kelly sat up in bed waiting, watching, wondering if, when she didn't show up at Dalton's door, he would come to her as he had before, through the secret passageway. She'd propped a chair up against the bookshelves, knowing it would clatter, alert her to his presence if he tried to come to her through the hidden stairway.

She picked up the script that Dalton had given her days before. Days... It seemed like months earlier that Dalton had come to talk to her when she'd been stripping the wallpaper. She thought of how his eyes had gleamed with keen intelligence, radiated with curiosity and optimism. She squeezed her eyes tightly closed

as the vision was usurped by the image of Dalton's
eyes the last time she'd seen him. Intense with a wildness that showed no intelligence, only radiating pure
emotion . . . a black emotion.

Was the Dalton she cared about gone forever?
Would Randolf's madness eventually consume Dalton's soul?

She shoved these thoughts away, finding them too
painful to contemplate. Instead she picked up the
script, curious as she read the title. *Silent Screams.*
Despite Malcolm's pronouncement that it was nothing but trash, Kelly opened the first page and began to
read.

It was nearly midnight when she finally finished the
script and placed it on the floor next to the bed. She
leaned her head back and frowned thoughtfully. As
far as she was concerned, the script had been powerful, tightly written, with a part that would have been
perfect for Randolf. The basic premise was that of a
man driving his brother insane. Who better to play the
part of the tortured madman but Randolf?

Of course, she wasn't an agent and was sure Malcolm had used his best judgment in turning down the
role for Randolf. Still, she couldn't help but wonder,
if Randolf had gotten a plum part, what that would
have done to change the course of fate.

She looked at the bookshelf that hid the secret passageway. Apparently Dalton wasn't going to use it tonight. Good. She had dreaded an argument with an
angry entity, but she definitely wasn't going to make
love with one, either.

The house was silent around her, not a creak or groan to indicate anyone awake anywhere. She reached over and turned off her light, then settled against her pillow, immediately feeling the soft waves of approaching sleep reaching out to her. . . .

She awoke suddenly, her gaze immediately shooting to the bookcase. In the moonlight streaming in through her window, she could see that the bookshelf and the chair remained in place. That hadn't been what had awakened her.

Looking at the luminous hands of her clock, she realized she'd been asleep no longer than half an hour. It wasn't quite one o'clock.

She remained still for a moment, wondering what had pulled her from her sleep. Then she heard it, the distant cry of her name.

Kelly. Kelly.

It wasn't an actual audible call, but rather a voice in her head, beseeching her, beckoning her. She instantly recognized it as Dalton. He needed her.

As if in a dream, she got out of bed, not bothering with a light. Using the moon to guide her, she slipped on her robe and left her room. Moving down the hallway toward the stairs, she felt an inexplicable dread tugging at her, demanding she turn and go back to her room, back to the safety of her own bed.

She ignored the feeling, instead following Dalton's soulcry. The stairs were nearly pitch-black and she used the banister to guide her slowly upward. It seemed to vibrate beneath her fingertips, and the feeling of dread intensified with each step she took. Still, she could not resist Dalton's evocative cries.

She reached the top of the staircase, hesitating for a moment. "Hello...is somebody there?" She had the distinct feeling of not being alone, of someone standing in the darkness next to her.

"Dalton...is that you?" she whispered. She reached out a hand, gasping as she was shoved hard in the chest. She stumbled backward, flailing her arms helplessly as she realized there was nothing but air beneath her feet. In horror she realized she was falling. Falling to her death, just like Daphne.

CHAPTER TWELVE

Kelly hit one step with her shoulder, bounced off another with her hip. The pain ricocheted through her as she reached desperately for the banister to break the fall.

Suddenly she felt a cloudlike softness beneath her, like a pillow cushioning her descent. Her nostrils filled with the scent of lilacs and with a soft thud she hit the carpet on the floor.

She lay unmoving. The pain in her hip and shoulder radiated through her and she wondered vaguely if she'd broken them both. She was disoriented, confused in the darkness. She knew she was at the bottom of the stairs, which meant she'd fallen down the entire flight. She should be dead. Perhaps she was. No, she hurt too badly to be dead, she decided.

She turned her head slightly, still smelling the strong scent of lilacs. Her eyes widened as in the heavy darkness she saw a vague mist gathering. The mist was lighter than the darkness and it swirled, beginning to gain form and definition. The scent of lilacs grew cloying, suffocating, as the vaporous mist spun itself into the form of a woman.

Kelly recognized her, and as the spirit leaned down, breathing its death-breath on Kelly's face, she screamed, and then there was nothing but darkness.

She came to moments later, the lights above her blazing in painful intensity. She snapped her eyes closed again against their assault.

"Don't move, Kelly." She recognized Gary's voice and cracked her eyelids open once again. Gary leaned over her, as did Susan, who clutched the middle of her sleep shirt like a nun worrying rosary beads. Jeffrey and Malcolm were there as well, Jeffrey bare-chested in a pair of jeans and Malcolm in a gray velour bathrobe that matched exactly the color of his hair.

Kelly tested her legs, moving them against the cold wooden floor. Her hip ached, but she realized there were no broken bones. "I'm...I'm all right," she said faintly, sitting up and grabbing her shoulder.

"You really shouldn't move until we can get a doctor to look at you," Gary protested.

"I don't need a doctor. Really, I'm fine." Her shoulder throbbed with an intensity that dried her mouth. She moved her arm experimentally, grimacing as she realized it was probably just bruised or sprained. "If somebody could just help me up."

Four pairs of hands reached for her, but it was Susan and Gary who pulled her up between them as Jeffrey and Malcolm looked on in concern.

"Kelly, what happened?" Susan asked, her eyes holding an edge of hysteria.

Kelly's gaze went back up the stairs, back to where shadows still clung in the hallway. She looked at Susan, saw the tenuous grip she had on her composure and forced a smile. "Oh, silly me. I tried to go upstairs in the dark and I guess I missed a step." Kelly tried to laugh, but it came out a low moan.

"You could have been killed," Susan exclaimed, her grip around Kelly's waist painfully tight. Still, Kelly didn't protest the grip; she welcomed the pain as a sign of blessed life.

"Those stairs should be torn out, rebuilt," Malcolm exclaimed. "They're far too steep for safety. They already claimed one life and now nearly another."

Kelly eased herself away from Susan and Gary. "I guess the excitement is over for tonight. I'm sorry I frightened you all, but we can all go back to bed now."

Susan frowned. "Are you sure? Maybe I should sit with you for a while. Did you bump your head at all?"

"No, my head is fine. Really, I'm fine," she assured them all. "Please, let's just call it a night."

It wasn't until everyone was back in their rooms and Kelly was in her bed that she allowed herself to think about what had happened.

Had she bumped her head? Is that what had caused the strange vision of Daphne to appear? Had that mistlike apparition only been an image created by the fall? She'd smelled the lilac odor before . . . that night when Dalton had made love to her and she knew he wasn't Dalton but Randolf. Had Daphne been there in the room? Hovering above? Watching as her husband's spirit had possessed Kelly's body?

Kelly pulled the blanket up more firmly around her neck, seeking warmth, wincing as her shoulder cried out in protest. She felt as if she'd never be warm again.

She frowned, replaying in her mind the events as they had happened. In her disorientation she might have imagined Daphne's spirit floating around her, the feel of a gravelike breath on her face, but she hadn't imagined the hand that had shoved her down the stairs. That was as real as the black-and-blue bruises forming on her body, as real as the softness of the bed beneath her.

Had it been an angry, vengeful Daphne who'd pushed her down the stairs? Then what had it been that had cushioned her fall? Something had drifted her down the flight of stairs, delivering her safely to the bottom. She should have been dead, but something had saved her life.

Yes, something had saved her life, but something—*or someone*—had tried to kill her.

She burrowed deeply beneath the blankets, cold terror coursing through her, twisting in the pit of her stomach. Nothing made any sense anymore. The rules of rational thinking no longer seemed to apply.

If the spirit of Daphne had saved her life, then who had tried to kill her? There was only one possible answer and her heart tried to deny the very probability.

Dalton. It had been his voice that had awakened her in the first place. It had been *his* call that had beckoned her up the stairs.

Had he been waiting for her in the shadows of the stairs? Had he led her up the stairs while he watched, waited? Waited for the opportune moment when a shove would send her reeling backward?

No, please. Not Dalton, her heart protested vehemently. Dalton wouldn't harm her. But Randolf would, and Randolf was in full possession of Dalton's body. At the moment, Randolf and Dalton were one and the same, and Kelly realized as long as that was the case, she had to fear them both.

"Kelly, come with us," Susan pleaded, her blue eyes darkened in worry.

"I can't." Kelly leaned against the front doorframe, her gaze going to Gary, who was putting boxes and suitcases in the trunk of their car.

"I feel like I'm a rat deserting a sinking ship," Susan said, worrying one of her curls to a frazzle. "I just can't stay here another minute, and you shouldn't either."

"This is my house, and I'm not going to be chased away by a crazy man in the attic or things that go bump in the night," Kelly returned firmly.

Susan placed a hand on Kelly's arm. "Kelly, this isn't your house. It's Randolf and Daphne's, and I think they want it back."

Kelly sighed and rubbed her aching shoulder. "No, I don't think it's the house they want. All I have to do is figure out what it is they *do* want, then they'll go away."

"After last night how can you even think of staying here another minute?" Susan asked incredulously. "Kelly, you could have been killed!"

"But I wasn't, and I should never have told you what really happened." Over coffee that morning, Kelly had shared with Susan all the events that had surrounded her fall down the stairs. She'd told her about the vicious shove, the feeling of floating, the lilac scent...everything. To Kelly's chagrin, Susan had immediately decided that she and Gary should move back into their Manhattan apartment.

"I'm sorry, Kelly, I just can't spend another night in this house."

"I understand, Susan. Really, I do." Kelly gave her friend a warm hug. "But you two will still come out here for my party?"

"You're still going to have it?" Again Susan's voice rose with incredulity.

Kelly merely nodded. There was absolutely no way she could explain to Susan that she *had* to give the party, that she felt it was a part of the puzzle that needed to be solved. "Will you come?"

Susan hesitated only a moment, then grinned. "I suppose even rats return to sinking ships if there's a party going on." She laughed and returned Kelly's hug. "We'll be here." She released Kelly and stared at her, the fear once again in her eyes. "Are you sure you won't come with us? I know it's a small apartment, but there's always room for a friend."

Kelly shook her head. "This is my home and this is where I'll stay. Besides, I've got to do something to help Dalton."

Susan's expression darkened and she twisted a strand of her hair between her fingers again. "That man is beyond help. If you won't come with us, then evict him. You didn't have any of us sign a lease, so you'd be within your rights. Kelly, the odds are good that it was him that pushed you down the stairs last night."

"I know," Kelly replied helplessly. "But it wasn't really him. It was something that's taken control of him."

"I think this house has possessed *you,*" Susan retorted, shivering as her gaze encompassed the structure that loomed above them.

Kelly stroked the wood of the doorway. "Perhaps it has," she agreed. She eyed Susan intently. "But I'm not leaving here and I'm not turning my back on Dalton."

They said their goodbyes, then Kelly watched as their car disappeared from sight. She walked back into the house, an unnatural stillness prevailing within the walls. It was as if Susan and Gary had taken with them what little lightness, what little natural noise, the house had contained.

Kelly wandered around the living room, noting how even in the brightness of morning light the house seemed to manufacture deep shadows that lingered in the corners, painted the hallway in somber grays and deep purples.

"Daphne!"

The cry shattered the silence, split apart the shadows and resounded in the hallway. Kelly stood still, staring up the stairs, up toward Dalton's room.

Her heart filled the silence that once again resumed, thudding with a rapidity that threatened to explode it out of her chest. The house seemed to close in around her as fingers of fear squeezed her from within.

"Daphne."

The cry came again, as brutal, as demanding, as terrifying as the first. It was followed by a loud crash, as if a piece of furniture had been flung against a wall.

Despite the overriding horror that swept through her, in spite of her fear for her own safety, she walked up the stairs, drawn there by a force she could neither ignore nor deny.

She felt his need pulling at her, and she didn't know if it was Randolf's need for Daphne, or Dalton's need for her. She only knew she had to answer the summons.

She paused just outside his door, her fingertips touching the wood. She drew back with a start, the energy pulsating through the door burning her. She jumped as again she heard a loud crash followed by a splintering noise. It sounded as if he was slowly, methodically destroying the room.

"Daphne." The cry seemed not to come from the mouth of a person, but rather from the very soul. It vibrated in the air with an unearthly resonance.

"Dalton," Kelly cried through the door. "Dalton, it's me." Once again she placed her hands on the door, wanting to connect with his soul, Dalton's soul.

There was a stillness in the air, as if all the psychic energy held its breath in anticipation.

"Dalton?"

"Kelly." Her name escaped him on a sigh and she knew he stood achingly close to the other side of the door. She felt his white energy seeping through the wood, radiating up her arms and into her heart.

"Dalton, open the door."

"No, I can't." She could hear his labored breathing, feel his deep anguish. "Kelly...I think I'm crazy. You must stay away from me...it's not safe for you. I'm no longer in control and there's such an anger inside me.... Please, just leave me alone." His voice rose in pitch and tone. "Leave me alone!"

Thunder crackled overhead and Kelly raced back down the stairs, fear tasting metallic in her mouth. She locked herself in her room and spent the next few minutes moving furniture against the bookshelf that hid the passageway. She grunted and groaned beneath the effort, each movement renewing the pain in her hip and shoulder. But she had to barricade the passageway. Dalton himself knew he might do something horrible. He'd warned her away from him.

He'd used the passageway once to come and take her love. The next time he used it he might be coming to take her life.

She didn't relax until she was positive there was enough weight against the shelf that it would take superhuman strength to move it. Even then she didn't feel secure. After all, a supernatural being might possess superhuman strength.

She jumped as a knock fell on her door. "Who— who is it?" she asked wildly.

"Umm, Kelly...it's me...Jeffrey."

She opened the door and resisted the impulse to throw herself in his arms, just needing somebody to hold her and tell her everything was all right.

"Are you all right?" he asked. "I heard a bunch of noise in here and wondered if everything was okay."

Kelly nodded. "I'm fine."

Jeffrey's gaze went over her shoulder, to the pile of furniture at the far end of her room. "You've got an unusual decorating style," he observed.

Kelly sighed and motioned him into the room, carefully locking the door behind them. "I owe it to you to tell you what's been going on. Who knows, you might be in some sort of danger, too." She motioned him to the table, where they both sat down. She told him about being shoved down the stairs the night before, about Dalton's possession, his possessiveness and jealous rages and his suspicions that Kelly and Jeffrey were involved romantically.

Jeffrey took it all in, nodding occasionally, showing the calm acceptance of youth. "I knew something weird was going on here. I've felt stuff, too."

"You have?" Kelly looked at him eagerly. There were times when she wondered if she was going mad, if she was the only one in the house sensing things that weren't there, the only one who felt the presence of ghosts and energies.

Jeffrey nodded. "I know it sounds crazy, but there have been several times I've awakened in the night and heard somebody singing me a lullaby. And always when that happens, I smell flowers."

"Daphne." Kelly breathed her name in a whisper, as if afraid saying it too loud would conjure up the spirit. She got up and stood at the window, staring out in frustration. "What can they want?"

"Why don't you ask them?"

She turned and looked at him. "What?"

"You know, a séance. Why don't you have one and ask the spirits what they want, why they're here."

"But that's crazy," she protested with a small hysterical giggle.

"No crazier than that." He pointed to the pile of furniture.

The hysterical giggle died and Kelly sobered. "A séance," she mused thoughtfully. "Don't you have to have a medium or something?"

"You could be the medium," Jeffrey said, leaning eagerly toward her. "I mean, it's obvious you've got some sort of psychic ability, and the spirits are already in contact with you in some way or another."

"I don't know...." She hesitated, remembering Susan's words of warning, of being in too deep, of losing her own soul. "The thought of a séance scares me."

"And you aren't scared now?" Jeffrey observed wryly.

Kelly laughed and looked at him with a new respect. "You're absolutely right. At this point I guess I've got nothing to lose."

"So we do it tonight?"

Kelly hesitated a long moment, then nodded.

"Terrific." He got up and went to the door. "Why don't we meet in the study at midnight? I'll bring the candles."

"And I'll bring the ghosts," Kelly added beneath her breath as he left.

She stood up and walked over to the window, staring out at the storm clouds overhead. Dark and heavy, they swallowed up the sun, swallowed up everything in their path.

It seemed as if every afternoon it stormed. The meteorologists talked about jet streams and tropical lows, but Kelly knew the turbulent skies were being fed by the tumultuous energies of the house. Kelly frowned and turned away from the window, wondering if, by having a séance, they weren't inviting the storm *into* the house.

It was five minutes to midnight when Kelly made her way to the study, afraid of what she and Jeffrey were about to do, yet afraid not to follow through on the plan.

He was already there, waiting for her, candles filling the room with fragrance and flickering light. She noticed the chill the moment she walked in. No, not a chill, but an unnatural bone-shivering cold.

"You feel it, too?" Jeffrey asked, looking like a kid anticipating a ride on a roller coaster.

She nodded, wondering if he had any idea of the danger they could be in by summoning spirits so possibly malevolent. "Maybe we should make a fire," she suggested, wrapping her arms around her shoulders to still the shivering.

He immediately set to the task, and within minutes a fire popped and sparked, casting long, eerie shadows on the walls. The fire didn't dispel the darkness, Kelly thought, moving nearer the flames, eager for the heat. Rather it seemed to create the darkness that lingered in the corners, casting flickers of light to cover the shadows like ineffectual veils.

"I brought some chalk," Jeffrey said, his sparkling eyes belying the solemn tones of his voice. "You and Susan talked about once using a Ouija board. I figured if you wanted we could make our own board here." He pointed to the top of the coffee table.

Kelly watched as Jeffrey moved the floral arrangement, then wrote on the top of the coffee table. With a stick of thick white chalk, he laid out the letters of the alphabet with the meticulous care of an artist. When he was finished, he grabbed a water glass and turned it upside down in the center of the game board he had created.

"Are we ready?" he asked, sitting on the floor and placing the fingertips of one hand on the top of the inverted glass.

Kelly wanted to scream no. No, she wasn't ready. She didn't want to make contact with dead people, converse with spirits. Still, if by following through on this madness she could gain some answers that might save Dalton's soul, then it was worth the fear that crawled in the pit of her stomach, and made her hands tremble uncontrollably.

She sat down on the floor across from Jeffrey and placed her fingertips on the top of the glass. Nothing happened. The fire hissed and snapped, the candlelight danced on the walls. But nothing out of the ordinary happened.

"We must be doing something wrong," Kelly finally whispered in frustration.

"Maybe we need to call to them," Jeffrey suggested. He cleared his throat. "If there are any spirits present, please show yourself."

Kelly gasped as the temperature of the room once again plummeted and the glass began moving erratically across the top of the coffee table. She pulled her hand away and stared at Jeffrey. "Did you move it?"

He shook his head vigorously, his eyes wide. "I think we made contact."

Kelly rubbed her hands together, staring at the glass with a mixture of awe and horrified fascination. She reached out her hand and once again put her fingers on the glass. Immediately she felt a palpable energy radiating from it. The glass moved rapidly from letter to letter, as if assessing the board.

"Ask it a question," Jeffrey prompted.

Kelly wet her lips, her mouth dry with fear. "Who...who are you?"

She watched as the glass shot across the letters, pausing on the ones it wanted. The air suddenly filled with the scent of sweet lilacs.

D-A-P-H-N-E.

Kelly gasped. Even though she'd known on some emotional level that Daphne's spirit still filled the house, seeing the name spelled out both stunned and frightened her.

The glass paused in the center of the table, as if awaiting the next question. "How did you die?" Kelly asked. The glass shot to the M, then to the U-R-D-E-R-E-D. Kelly watched in fascination as the spirit of Daphne answered the question.

MURDERED.

"How did Randolf die?" Jeffrey asked, but the glass didn't move. He looked at Kelly. "It's only answering you."

"How did Randolf die?" Kelly repeated the question, watching intently as the glass whirled around and around the board, pausing hesitantly over the S, then firing off to spell out M-U-R-D-E-R-E-D.

Kelly jerked her hand off the glass and stared at Jeffrey in confusion. "Murdered? Why did it say that? He committed suicide. Maybe she's confused. Maybe she misunderstood the question."

"Don't ask me—ask it again," Jeffrey replied, his gaze intent on the glass.

She placed her hand back on the glass. "Did Randolf commit suicide?" The glass spun around and around the board, as if agitated, then pointed to the word *no* and once again spelled *murdered*.

"Who murdered you? Who murdered Randolf?" Kelly leaned forward intently, aware that the answers Dalton had sought might be here beneath her fingertips.

Again the glass moved wildly and paused at the *M*, then blasted across to the no, then yes, then around and around the alphabet.

Kelly felt the erratic energy coursing from her fingers up through her arm, out of control. It was out of control. EVILHEREEVILHEREEVILHERE.

The cold of the room seeped into Kelly's heart, her soul, filling her with horror as she realized what the spirit was saying. *Evil here.* She felt a sheen of perspiration on her face, the arctic air of the room making it feel like a blanket of ice. A loud clap of thunder boomed overhead, followed by a strike of lightning so close to the house it raised the hair on the back of Kelly's neck.

She felt the room spinning with a psychic energy that was definitely out of control. The flames in the fireplace shot up the chimney, as if a cupful of gasoline had been poured onto the fire.

"Why are you still here?" Kelly asked, fighting her need to break the contact, to pull her fingers off the transmitting glass. The tumbler pirouetted and revolved with a quickness that made it difficult for them to keep up with it.

TOWARNTOWARNTOWARN.

To warn? Kelly frowned and looked at Jeffrey, but he seemed to be in a world of his own, his eyes focused hypnotically on the glass. "To warn who? Who's in danger?" she asked.

She stared in horror as the glass whirled to the letters, slowly spelling out the answer.

KELLYKELLYKELLYKELLY.

CHAPTER THIRTEEN

"Daphne."

The bellow came from the attic, followed by a clap of thunder that shook the rafters. Kelly looked upward, shivering as she recognized the utter madness in Dalton's voice.

Lightning slashed the semidarkness of the room. A gust of wind swirled inside the study and snuffed out the candles with unnatural intent. The fire seemed to capture the candle flames, glowing with an unnatural brightness for a single instant, then dying back down to smoldering embers resembling alien eyes.

Kelly felt the energy leave the glass and her fingertips. She cried out in protest. "Wait . . . Daphne," she called frantically. "Don't go. Come back. Please come back. I need you."

Silence. The glass no longer shimmered beneath her touch. The temperature of the air slowly warmed. The scent of lilacs was gone, leaving behind only the odor of the wood burning in the fireplace and the smell of Kelly's own fear.

"It's gone," Jeffrey observed, his voice soft with awe. He rose from the floor and turned on the lamp on top of the bar.

Kelly got up and sat down on the love seat, trying to still the shivering that shook her uncontrollably.

She stared at the coffee table, where Jeffrey's chalk-drawn alphabet remained. The letters of her name were smeared from where the glass had zoomed to them over and over again.

KELLYKELLYKELLY.

If the spirit that had spoken to them through the makeshift Ouija board was really Daphne, then according to what she'd said, she was here to warn Kelly she was in danger. But danger from who... or what? From Dalton?

"Maybe we should try to contact her again," Kelly said hopefully. "Maybe she'll come back."

Jeffrey shrugged his shoulders. "I'm game if you are." He shut off the light and relit the candles, then once again positioned himself on the floor.

Kelly joined him and together they placed their fingertips on the top of the glass. Kelly called to Daphne, pleaded with the spirit woman to return, but nothing happened.

"It's no use," she said fifteen minutes later. "She's not coming back." Black despair welled up inside her, mingling with the taste of fear.

She watched as Jeffrey blew out the candles and once again turned on the bar lamp, the illumination unable to pierce the sweeping darkness within that threatened to engulf her.

"Are you all right?" Jeffrey asked, his eyes lit with concern.

Kelly nodded. "As right as I can be considering I've just been warned by a spirit that I'm in danger."

"Whew, it's been quite a night," Jeffrey agreed, tugging nervously on the tiny gold hoop in his ear. "So, what do you think?"

Kelly sighed and shivered once again, cold despite the warmth that now filled the study. "I don't know what to think," she admitted. "I didn't get any real answers." She rubbed her forehead with two fingers. "I'm just so confused."

"Daphne said that she and Randolf were murdered by evil," Jeffrey began, his brow wrinkled in deep thought. "Is it possible that Randolf was possessed, too? That maybe instead of him being totally bonkers, it was a possession by some evil entity that caused him to kill Daphne, then himself?"

Kelly looked at him in surprise, letting the possibility roll over her. Was it possible? And was it that same evil entity that now had a hold on Dalton?

There was one other possibility.... Could somebody on the night of that party so long ago have killed both Randolf and Daphne? Or maybe it had just been an accident—Daphne had accidently fallen down the stairs. But how could something that happened so long ago put Kelly in jeopardy? It made no sense. None of this made any sense.

"I think I'll call it a night," she said, rising. Although she knew sleep would be a long time in coming, she needed to be alone to think.

As she went to her room, her head ached with suppositions and possibilities. Only one thing remained pure and simple. Something wanted to harm her, and it was working through Dalton. She felt danger spinning in the air around her, as palpable as the walls surrounding her.

She thought again of the party she'd planned and knew she should cancel it. First thing in the morning she would write out cancellation notes to everyone who'd been invited.

She started to reach for the antique silk nightgown, then changed her mind. The one and only time she'd worn it had been that night of swirling, mindless passion, the night when Randolf had come to her and made love to her as if she was Daphne.

Clad in her pink nightgown, she crawled into bed, eyeing the furniture barricade against the bookshelf. What was she going to do? She was living with a man who scared her to death. In the daylight, knowing Jeffrey and Malcolm were around, she could keep her fear of Dalton at bay.

But at night, when darkness shrouded the world, there seemed no way to chase away thoughts of the boogeyman...and the boogeyman had the face of the man she loved.

She froze as the full extent of her feelings for Dalton swept through her. *Love.* Yes, that was what they had been building before this madness had set in. Tears burned in her eyes as she thought of Dalton, of what they might have had. She'd waited twenty-seven years to find the man she knew she loved...only to discover he was possessed by an evil entity.

But was it a love destined to end in her death? Dear God, what did Randolf want? Why were he and Daphne still here?

Getting into bed, she pulled the blankets up tightly around her neck. She remembered the lighthearted vow she'd made to Dalton on the morning after they had made love. "I'll fight your demons," she'd said.

But what frightened her more than anything was the foreboding feeling that Dalton's demons were dark monsters, far too powerful for her love to fight.

Dawn finally brought exhausted sleep. Kelly had been unable to surrender to rest with the world concealed in tenebrous hues and her heart layered with tiers of fear and dread. It was only when the pale morning light seeped in through the window that she was finally able to give in to the vulnerability of unconscious sleep.

It was nearly noon when she awoke, feeling as if she'd spent the entire night wrestling phantom ghosts with evil laughter and blackened hearts.

She showered and dressed, then opened her door, looking first left, then right. She didn't want to encounter Dalton unexpectedly, yet she wanted to see him more than anyone on earth.

Silence. The house seemed shrouded in it. She leaned against the doorframe and listened to the emptiness. She suddenly felt so alone. She hadn't realized until now just how lonely her life had been since the death of her grandmother.

For all too brief a time, Dalton had filled up the emptiness, chased away the loneliness. She'd had a momentary glimpse of what they might have shared together, then it had been cruelly snatched away.

She looked up the stairs, wondering what he was doing. She didn't know what terrorized her more—the loud banging and noise or the profound silence that radiated upstairs. At least when there was pandemonium issuing from the room she knew he was up there. With the silence came the trepidation of trying to guess where he would silently appear, bringing with him the distinguishing bay rum scent that provoked goose bumps of dread on her skin.

A whisper of movement drifted up to her, and her gaze shifted down the stairs to the study doorway. She caught a glimpse of Malcolm's back as he disappeared into the room.

She knew she should go down and see if he was looking for her, but she was reluctant to leave the relative safety of her own space. The memory of the séance, the warnings, Randolf's anguished cries for his long-dead lover were still too fresh in her mind. She wasn't ready to return to the study. Not yet. If Malcolm was looking for her, he would know to come to her room.

She closed the door, feeling a certain amount of safety being in her locked room. Although she knew locked doors couldn't keep out ghosts and supernatural entities, it could keep out Dalton's physical presence.

Grabbing a box of stationery, she sat down at the table. She had to get the cancellation notices in the mail today if she wanted everyone to receive them before the night of the party.

She picked up her ballpoint pen, doodling with it until the ink ran in a flowing blue, then she picked up a piece of stationery and began to write. Immediately the ink quit flowing. Sighing in irritation, she once again moved the tip in whirls on a piece of scrap paper, frowning as the ink began again to roll in the appropriate, precise flow.

Once again she guided the tip of the pen to the top of the stationery, but before she could touch it to the paper, the pen flew out of her hand, landing inches away.

Dread coursed through her as the scent of lilacs filled the room. She looked around, her eyes widened as she sought a vision of the ghostly woman. Kelly could hear the soft click of the clock on the dresser as one...two...three minutes ticked by and nothing happened. There was no swirling mist, no strange fog. Only the sweet floral smell alerted her that something was amiss. "Daphne?" she whispered aloud. Two more minutes passed and still nothing occurred. The scent remained, faint and haunting.

Kelly picked up the pen once again, but this time when she tried to guide it to the stationery she felt a counterpressure working against her, keeping the pen's tip from touching the paper. Kelly exerted more pressure, but it was impossible for her to overcome the power working against her. The scent of lilacs grew stronger and the box of stationery spilled to the floor. Kelly released her hold on the pen and it flew across the room, landing on the floor near her bed.

"Okay," she said shakily. She knew what Daphne was trying to tell her. "Okay. I won't cancel the party."

Immediately the smell dissipated, then disappeared altogether, and Kelly knew she was once again alone in the room. So Daphne wanted the party to take place. A party had played a role in the tragedy that had unfolded so many years before, Kelly thought. It was as if Randolf and Daphne wanted to recreate the past and play out the drama once again. A wave of apprehension swept through her. The only difference between the past drama and this one was that in this one she and Dalton had the lead roles.

She suddenly needed to be out of the house. The walls pressed in with claustrophobic intensity. She left her room and went downstairs. Without looking left or right, she hurried through the study and out the back door. She skirted the stone bench on the patio and walked toward the shoreline.

The autumn sunlight was warm on her shoulders, although the breeze danced impishly with a cool nip that portended the winter to come.

Would she even be here for winter? Or would somebody else have bought the house, intrigued by the mirror of tragedies the place had seen?

She sat down on the sand, chiding herself for her morbid thoughts. She wasn't about to become a tragedy, a helpless victim to a mad ghost. She'd told Dalton she'd be his light in the darkness, but his darkness was too powerful, too murky with mysteries she couldn't fathom.

Dalton was lost and so was she if she couldn't figure out what the ghosts from the past wanted, what had brought them back to this place and time.

"You should be doing things to prepare for our party. What are you doing out here?"

The deep voice spun her around, and her heart jumped into her throat as she saw Dalton looming above her. With the sun at his back, his face was cast in shadowed darkness, his features obscured into a black mask. But she could see the glittering intensity of his deranged gaze.

She stood up and faced him, her hands trembling as she brushed away the sand that clung to the seat of her jeans. "I was thinking about you," she answered truthfully, fear racing through her veins as rapidly as her blood.

"How touching. Do you also think of me when you're making love to all those others?"

Kelly didn't bother to answer. She knew nothing she said could assuage the jealousy that ate him up inside. In any case, she couldn't have answered him. Her throat had gone completely dry at his unexpected appearance.

"Ah, my love. How did we come to such a mess?" There was a weary resignation in his voice that somehow frightened her more than the overbrilliance of his eyes, more than the possessive rage he'd shown her before. He sat down on the sand and gestured for her to sit next to him.

With her heart still a lump in her throat, she sat down. Even with inches between them and no physical contact whatsoever, she felt surrounded by his field of energy. Raw and powerful, it made breathing difficult.

"What happened to us? We had it all." His voice was soft, filled with a wistful yearning that pulled at Kelly despite her fear of him. "Where did it go so wrong?" He reached out and took her hand. His own was cold, as if bloodless, and a frosty sensation traveled up Kelly's arm, encasing her heart in ice.

"I know things haven't been easy lately." His gaze played on her intently. "And I know there are times when you're afraid of me. But you needn't be afraid. I love you, Daphne."

His words caused the ice crystals around Kelly's heart to melt into tears. Oh, how she would have reveled in those words if they had been spoken to her with Dalton's heart, Dalton's soul.

He stood, his hand pulling her up beside him. He looked out at the ocean waves pounding their eternal rhythm against the shore. He gazed back at her, a new madness darkening the abyss of his eyes. "If it were just you and me, we'd be all right." He ran one hand across his eyes, as if trying to clear away cobwebs that obscured reality. His other hand kept a firm grip on her.

"You and me...together through eternity...one with the sand and the sea and the sky." He spoke as if in a hypnotic trance and as he talked, he pulled her closer and closer to the pounding waves. His gaze didn't waver from some point in the distance . . . some vision that only he saw.

The ocean water swirled at Kelly's feet, seeping through her canvas shoes. Cold. The water was the temperature of a moist grave, and she suddenly realized his intent as he continued walking, pulling her into the icy waves.

"Together forever . . . with nobody to tell me of your indiscretions. Just you and me existing forever in each other's embrace. We'll escape this madness, escape the world."

Kelly struggled against his tight clutch, the water caressing her calves, reaching up for her knees. "Dalton," she protested, yanking, fighting against him. The arctic water lapped at her thighs, as if hungry to consume her completely, and Dalton's mad chant of togetherness continued as he drew her farther and farther into the watery grave.

"Dalton, please . . ." she cried out. "For God's sake, *I'm not Daphne. I'm Kelly.* You aren't Randolf."

He hesitated, his fixed stare moving from the distance to her. Confusion mingled with madness, then transformed to horror. "Kelly?" His features crumpled into despair. "Kelly . . . run," he whispered hoarsely.

She twisted from his grip and stumbled back from him. "Dalton?"

"Run." He yelled, the cry coming from someplace deep within him, radiating with such torment it moved her to comply.

She ran with a panicked desperation, her wet shoes and jeans impeding her. She didn't stop until she was at the back door, then she turned and stared at him. He still stood in the breaking waves, like an avenging Neptune. As she watched he flung his head back. *"Daphne!"* he screamed, and she knew he was back in the world of his madness.

"Daphne...let me in." The whisper drifted through the barricaded passageway, soft and poignant, haunting in its longing.

Kelly remained in bed, staring at the barrage of furniture against the bookshelf, hoping, praying, it would be strong enough to keep him out.

"Daphne ... I'm sorry. I didn't mean to frighten you. You know I could never hurt you. I love you." A sob caught in his throat. "I just don't know what to do anymore. I don't know what's happening to me ... to us."

Kelly didn't answer him, not wanting to feed the frenzied emotion, knowing there was little she could say to comfort a ghost.

"If only he'd leave me alone. He comes in my study and when he does bugs crawl on the walls and my face melts and I see hell." His voice took on the raving tones of madness, and Kelly clamped her hands over her ears, not wanting to hear any more.

"He whispers to me of your cheating and he tells me you don't really love me. He tells me you're going to leave me forever." His voice rose hysterically. "And the walls change colors and the ceiling closes in and the bugs are everywhere...everywhere. And I can't make them go away." His breath caught on another sob, and for a long moment she heard nothing but his labored breathing.

"Kelly... open the door."

The voice was Dalton's, soft and provocative, and Kelly pulled her hands down from her ears, her heart responding with a rapid beating. "Dalton?" She got out of bed and ran to the obstructed bookcase.

"Kelly... open the door. I need your help."

The soft, hypnotic tones called to her, beckoned her to do his bidding, but she fought against the mesmerizing pull.

"Kelly... please. Please open the door. I need you so badly."

Still she hesitated, torn between her need—her love—for Dalton and her fear of Randolf. "Dalton, tell me what to do," she cried. "Tell me what to do to help you. I don't know how."

"The first thing you can do is open the door. We need to be together. Please, Kelly. I love you."

Kelly remained unmoving, pausing as she tried to figure out what to do. Her hands trembled with the need to rip the furniture away from the bookcase, open the secret passageway and fall into Dalton's arms. She touched the dresser that rested against the hidden doorway. *Dalton,* her heart cried. *Dalton, what should I do?* But still she hesitated, uncertainty rippling through her.

She jumped and screamed as he hit the doorway with the raging power of a sledgehammer. "Damn you, open the door. You're my wife." Bang after bang vibrated the door as he shouted his wrath at being locked out. The furniture stacked against the bookcase shuddered with each blow, threatening to splinter apart beneath the assault.

Anger swelled inside her as she realized he'd tried to trick her. It hadn't been Dalton at all. "Why are you doing this? Leave him alone. Go back to where you came from." She shrieked her own rage back at him, crying in fear, in heartache, as she wondered if Dalton was truly gone forever, if he was beyond saving from the monster inside him.

She beat with her fists on top of the dresser, feeling helpless and trapped by things she couldn't fight. "What do you want? Just tell me why you're here. What do you want?"

A sudden silence fell in the room, as if time itself paused. Kelly crumpled to the floor, her rage spent, hopeless despair washing over her.

"You know what I want." The voice was once again soft . . . filled with such sad yearning. The haunting quality sent a deep shiver through Kelly's soul. "I want you . . . for eternity," the voice whispered.

CHAPTER FOURTEEN

Kelly stared at her reflection in the dresser mirror. She looked like a ghost. Pale, with dark shadows of exhaustion beneath her eyes, she looked as if she was slowly transforming into one of the pale wraithlike spirits that infested the house.

Every night for the past week she'd been barraged in the night by Dalton's whispers, his ranting, his rages vented through the passageway door. During the days there had been an ominous silence radiating from the upstairs, as if he needed to regain his strength for the witching hours of the night. And it was at night that the madness escaped, and always... always it sought her.

She wondered how Malcolm and Jeffrey were dealing with the eerie silences and nighttime ravings, but since she didn't leave her quarters and heard no sounds to indicate they left theirs, she had no way of knowing if they were even aware of the horrors she was experiencing.

She turned away from the mirror with a tired sigh and ran her hands nervously down the sides of her sleek, black dress. She had a man possessed by the ghost of a madman in her attic and thirty people coming in an hour's time for a housewarming party.

Ludicrous. The entire thing was ludicrous. She should have invited an exorcist. *That* would have been the crowning glory to the macabre gathering.

She'd tried to cancel the whole thing. Every day she had picked up the phone and tried to call the invited guests. But each time the phone had quit working and the room had filled with the odor of lilacs. Kelly finally resigned herself to the fact that she was no longer in control.

That morning, when she'd awakened, she'd immediately been aware of the pulsating energy in the air. It was as if all the psychic energy had converged, all the planets had aligned to create enough force to play out the drama of the night.

Kelly was helpless, unable to prepare herself for whatever the night would bring. How could one prepare for a night of madness, where reality was merely an illusion and spirits of the dead were in control?

Taking a deep breath, she left her room and sneaked down the stairs to the living room. The velvet sofa had been delivered the day before. With the original coffee table that had been in the basement polished and gleaming before it, and the new wallpaper decorating the walls, the room was taking shape.

She whirled around as she heard movement behind her, sighing in relief at the sight of Jeffrey standing in the doorway.

"The caterers left just a few minutes ago. They put everything out on a table in the dining room."

"Thank you for taking care of that for me." She smiled at the young man. Jeffrey had been a godsend in the past week, helping her pull together the party that shouldn't be happening.

"Are you all right?" he asked with concern.

She gave him a crooked smile of bravado. "Sure, I've just decided the best way to survive the night is to stay away from the stairs. If I'm not anywhere near them, then I can't fall down them."

Jeffrey nodded soberly. "How about if I move my stereo system in here? We can play some nice party background music."

"Sure, that would be great," Kelly agreed, again thinking of how ill-prepared she was for a festive night.

He turned to leave, but hesitated in the doorway, his eyes holding a reflection of the apprehension that stormed through Kelly. "Why don't we just lock him in that room for the night?"

"Jeffrey, you know as well as I do that none of this makes any rational kind of sense. My logic tells me you're right. The best way to handle this situation is to lock Dalton in his room for the duration of the party. But logic has no place in this house anymore." Kelly suddenly smelled the now-familiar odor of sweet flowers. She looked sharply at Jeffrey.

He nodded. "Yeah, I smell it. She's here. It's stronger than ever."

"And that's why I can't lock Dalton up."

"Is there anything I can do?" he asked.

Kelly shook her head. "I don't think so. Somehow I think this battle of souls is between Randolf and me. I don't know why he wants Dalton, but I want him more." She flushed as she heard the angry vehemence in her own voice.

As Jeffrey left to get his stereo, Kelly sat down on the edge of the sofa and looked up, as if trying to pierce the ceilings overhead and gaze directly into Dalton's room. What she'd told Jeffrey was true. Randolf might need Dalton's body for whatever nefarious purpose, but Kelly needed Dalton's heart, his soul, because she loved him. Was love stronger than evil? In the movies it always was, but this wasn't a movie and Kelly knew there were many times that evil overcame good. Was love powerful enough to battle Randolf? She had a feeling she would know that answer before this ordeal was over.

"Ah, there you are, my dear." Kelly stood up as Malcolm entered the living room, looking splendidly refined in a black suit. "I see you're all ready for your guests to arrive. I'm so looking forward to these walls embracing a party once again." He tilted his head sideways, gazing at her for just a moment, his brow wrinkled in slight confusion. "I... At this moment for some reason you remind me so of Daphne." His frown deepened as if he couldn't quite capture what it was that bothered him. Kelly knew. The room was still rife with Daphne's scent. Subconsciously Malcolm must be making the connection.

"It must be the dress," he finally said, his frown disappearing. "Yes, that must be it. She wore black at the party that night."

Kelly clutched her fingers into the skirt of the dress. Daphne had worn black... and Kelly had chosen the same, even though she had several other dresses that would have been appropriate.

Initially, she'd decided to wear it because she knew it looked terrific on her. With long, fitted sleeves and a plunging draped neckline, the dress emphasized her slender waist and the slight billow of skirt always made her feel feminine and sexy. However, she didn't feel sexy at the moment. Her mouth was dry as she wondered if she had involuntarily chosen her burial dress.

She shivered, the silk dress suddenly feeling cold, clinging to her in an unnatural fashion. She plucked at the skirt once again.

"The room looks nice," Malcolm observed. He walked over and stroked his gnarled hand across the back of the velvet sofa. "You're successfully keeping with the decor that was once here. I think Randolf and Daphne would have been pleased."

Kelly bit down on her bottom lip. Since that day on the beach, she hadn't tried to convince Malcolm that Dalton was possessed. The old man was confident in his mind that Dalton was crazy. She looked at him curiously. "Malcolm, you say you believe that Dalton has fallen into the same insanity that gripped Randolf, but I get the feeling that you aren't afraid of him."

Malcolm smiled enigmatically. "Why should I be afraid of him? Randolf was a danger only to himself... and, of course, to the woman he loved. It's the same with Dalton. I saw him only a little while ago at the top of the stairs." Malcolm leaned over and touched Kelly's arm sympathetically. "The man you knew as Dalton is gone. I don't know why exactly he's taken on the persona of his grandfather, but he's not in touch with reality at all."

"I just feel that if I can solve the mystery of what happened between Randolf and Daphne, then Dalton will be released from whatever it is that has a hold on him."

Malcolm's eyes blazed with unexpected intensity. "There is no mystery, Kelly. Leave the past alone." His hand shook on the back of the sofa and he released a soft sigh. "Just leave it all alone."

"I'd love to," Kelly returned softly. "But the past won't leave Dalton *or* me alone." She was interrupted by the ringing of the doorbell.

"Ah, the first guests have arrived," Malcolm said. "And so the party begins."

"Yes, and so the party begins," Kelly echoed faintly as she went to answer the door.

Over the next half hour the constant ring of the doorbell kept Kelly busy. But even the friendly faces and warm embraces of old friends and acquaintances couldn't remove the chill of quiet panic that fluttered in her veins.

Despite the crowd of people all talking and laughing, a pall of quiet permeated the house, as if the walls absorbed some of their chatter, stole pieces of their laughter. Despite the many people, there was a distinct chill in the air, one that Kelly knew the furnace couldn't warm.

Kelly walked from group to group, attempting to be a gracious hostess, but her thoughts focused on the man upstairs. Maybe nothing would happen tonight, she thought hopefully. Maybe Dalton wouldn't even attend the party. Yet she felt the supernatural energy crackling in the room, was aware of the pungent odor of bay rum and lilacs mingling with the other people smells and she knew that sooner or later the spirit lovers would be in complete control of the night.

A small smile tugged at her lips as she saw Jeffrey standing in a corner talking to a young receptionist from one of the doctors' offices that used Kelly's computer program. Good. She'd specifically invited the young girl with Jeffrey in mind.

Oh sure, she was a great matchmaker for others, but unfortunately the knack didn't extend to her own personal life. She, after all, had fallen in love with a man possessed by an evil ghost. The prognosis wasn't terrific for a happy ever after. She shoved her edge of black humor aside, recognizing it as a form of controlled hysteria.

"Hey, girl. Did I tell you that you look like hell?"

Kelly laughed. "Thanks, Susan, you sure know how to lift the spirits."

"Speaking of spirits..." Susan's eyebrows lifted, and she glanced upward. "How's Mr. Spirit himself?"

"Worse," Kelly admitted. She started to tell Susan all that had happened since she and Gary had moved out...Dalton's rages, the middle-of-the-night whispers, her overwhelming sense that things were coming to a climax.

She wanted to talk to Susan about everything, but she stopped herself. She could see by her expression that her friend didn't want to hear, didn't want to know. "Did you find the food?" she asked with forced brightness. "The caterers did a wonderful job with everything."

"That's just where I was headed," Susan replied, a look of relief sweeping over her features. "Want to join me?"

Kelly shook her head. "You go ahead. I'm going to mingle." As Susan disappeared, Kelly spied Byron Connors, the local news reporter who'd written an article about Kelly and the house when she'd first bought it.

"Nice gathering," he observed as she approached him. "The place sure looks different from the first time I was out here."

"It's amazing what a few carpenters and a lot of sweat can do," Kelly replied with a small smile.

"You know, a lot of the kids in the area used to think this place was haunted."

Kelly couldn't help the laughter that bubbled out of her. "Oh, Byron, you don't know the half of it," she exclaimed.

His brown eyebrows quirked up and his reporter nose twitched with what Kelly knew was the scent of a story. "So tell me."

She shook her head. Telling Susan was one thing, but telling Byron would be like broadcasting to the world that she was a loony-tune.

"I hear you've got Malcolm Jennings living here," Byron said.

"Yes, he's been helping another one of my tenants write a book on Randolf Weathers."

Again Byron's eyebrows danced upward. "I'm surprised he'd ever want to do that again after the Mesker fiasco."

"What fiasco?" Kelly asked. "I know the book did very well."

"Yeah, well, unfortunately the author didn't. He went crazy and committed suicide."

Kelly stared at him in surprise. "He *what?*"

Byron frowned. "I don't remember all the details. I know it was very soon after the book was published. There was some talk about drug abuse, but I don't think it was ever proved. From what I do remember, he just went nuts, seeing things and hearing voices. He jumped out of his apartment-building window." Byron looked at Kelly. "If you're really interested about the details, you should ask Malcolm Jennings. I think he was living with Mesker at the time."

Kelly looked across the room, where Malcolm was entertaining a small group of people, his wrinkled face wreathed with pleasure. Odd. Malcolm had lived with Randolf, and Randolf had gone crazy, shot his wife and then himself. The old man had lived with Gregory Mesker and he'd gone insane and jumped out an apartment window. Now Malcolm lived here and Dalton was crazy. An odd twist of fate? A coincidence? If so, it was an ominous one, but one that made no sense.

A hush suddenly fell over the group, and Kelly felt a renewed burst of energy pulsating in the air. As she followed the crowd's gaze to the top of the stairs, all her troubling thoughts of Malcolm flew out of her head.

Standing at the top of the stairs, his hair slicked back and emphasizing the hollows of his cheeks, was Dalton. He was dressed all in black, and never had he looked more like his grandfather. Power surrounded him, dark and vibrating, shimmering in the air and giving him the appearance of a magician who had appeared out of thin air through black magic.

He descended the stairs like a king in his palace, his gaze finding Kelly, consuming her with dark intensity. She wanted to run, to hide, but almost as if in a dream she went to him, meeting him at the bottom of the staircase. "Hello, darling. I'm glad you decided to join us." She knew she spoke the words, but she also knew the words hadn't come from her. It was a frightening feeling, the knowledge that something was inside her, working through her.

He smiled, the devastating smile that had sent women reeling in the aisles of movie theaters. "What kind of a host would I be if I spent my time up in my office during a party?" He placed an arm around her shoulder, pulling her against the heat that radiated from him. "Come, introduce me to your friends."

For Kelly, the next hour passed in a haze of unreality. Dalton remained at her side, his arm possessively around her, his heated gaze never wavering from her. There was a part of her that fought a shudder of revulsion, knowing that it wasn't Dalton who held her so tightly against his side, it wasn't his eyes that devoured her. But there was another part of her that wanted to fall into the fires that lit the very center of his dark irises, wanted to remain in his embrace for an eternity.

The air surrounding them seemed thinner, made breathing more difficult, and she felt slightly dizzy. The guests apparently felt the uncomfortable power crackling in the air, sensed something was amiss, something dangerous and unbridled. One by one, they said their goodbyes, subdued and seeming anxious to be away. She was pleased that Jeffrey and the young receptionist had definitely hit it off. Jeffrey left with the young woman to drive her home.

As Kelly showed the last of the guests out the door, she realized Dalton was no longer beside her. He'd disappeared, and his absence filled Kelly with a sense of impending doom.

She hadn't been so afraid when he'd been standing next to her in a room full of people. But now, with the silence of the house surrounding her and his whereabouts unknown, she was filled with an overriding terror. Where was Malcolm? She felt so alone and so vulnerable.

She walked around the living room, picking up empty glasses and paper plates, trying not to notice how the shadows gyrated and danced on the walls. The silence in the house was profound, broken only by the rapid beating of her own heart.

"Daphne." The cry drifted down the stairs, raising the hairs on the back of Kelly's neck. The paper plates she'd held in her hands fell to the floor and she began to shiver. *"Daphne...come to me."*

"Don't go up the stairs. Don't go up the stairs." She repeated the words like a mantra of protection. She wasn't going to allow the past to repeat itself. She refused to die the same kind of senseless death that Daphne had suffered. She would not fall down a flight of stairs.

"Daphne." A hint of suppressed anger rang in his voice. *"Don't make me angry. Don't make me come down there and find you."*

Kelly felt trapped. She stood in the center of the living room, waiting for Daphne to tell her what to do. Surely Daphne had had a plan for this night. Surely she'd had some plan in mind, some reason for allowing the party to take place, a motivation for letting the energies of the house reach the dimensions of no return. "Dammit, Daphne, you've been a thorn in my side for the past week. Where are you when I need you?" Kelly whispered. There was no reply, nothing, not even the sweet scent of the dead woman's perfume.

"Daphne!" Dalton's voice thundered with rage.

At the same time, Kelly saw out of the corner of her eye, Malcolm's diminutive form disappearing into the study. Kelly hesitated only a moment before hurrying after him. Surely with Malcolm present she'd be safer than she was alone.

She went into the study and looked around in confusion. The fire that had been lit earlier hissed softly in the grate, but other than that there was no noise, no sign of life. The room was empty. "But I know I saw him come in here," she murmured. She remembered another time when the same thing had happened. She'd chalked that first incident up to a mistake on her part. But tonight she knew she wasn't mistaken. Malcolm had entered the room only moments before her and now he was nowhere to be found.

On tiptoe she crossed to the door that led out to the beach, wondering if he'd gone outside, but the door was locked from the inside, so she knew he hadn't passed through it. Again a chill of apprehension raced up her spine and a sense of unreality veiled her perceptions.

Malcolm was no ghost. He didn't have the ability to pass through walls. Again she thought of the strange coincidence Byron had brought to her attention. She knew there was a connection, but she was unable to grasp its significance.

"Daphne." Dalton bellowed once again. This time his voice was stronger, closer than it had been earlier. He was coming down the stairs, coming for her.

Kelly looked around the room wildly, her gaze lingering on the bookcase by the fireplace. Something about it bothered her, didn't look quite right. She frowned, studying it, fighting down the sense of panic that threatened to overwhelm her.

Crooked. The bookshelves weren't flush against the wall. They protruded a mere inch, but it was an inch that screamed in Kelly's head. The secret passageway that ran from her room to Dalton's was hidden by a bookcase. Was it possible this was another one?

Kelly hurried to the shelf and pulled on it, gasping when it swung open easily. Behind it was a dark, narrow stairway. Where did it go? Panic still pumped through Kelly's veins. Did Dalton know about this secret stairway? Was it a dead end? Would she slip in here only to be trapped by Dalton, helpless against a murderous, evil ghost?

As Dalton yelled once again, and she heard his footsteps lumbering loudly down the stairs, Kelly ducked into the passageway, her heart pounding with an explosive rhythm. With fear that nearly blinded her, she pulled the bookshelf back in place, enclosing herself in the tomblike darkness.

CHAPTER FIFTEEN

The darkness surrounding her was profound, deep and frightening. The walls pressed against her with claustrophobic narrowness. She took a step up, biting back a squeal as a cobweb brushed her face with feathery fingers. She batted it away and climbed up the steep stairs. She used her hands like a blind person, feeling first the walls on the sides, then holding them out before her.

She moved soundlessly, the stairs not creaking or groaning, not making a single noise. From the study behind her she heard Dalton crying Daphne's name over and over again in impotent rage. She kept going up, distancing herself from the wrath of the entity behind her, hoping she wouldn't find herself ensnared between him and a sturdy wall.

She climbed the final step, finding herself against a barrier. She felt to the left, then to the right, but she was surrounded by walls. There was no place left to go.

She pushed on the wall in front of her. The claustrophobic sensation ebbed slightly as she felt a give. She pressed harder, wincing as she applied her sore shoulder to the task. Noiselessly the wall gave way. She blinked against the bright light and stepped into Dalton's room.

Malcolm stood directly before her, his back to her as his fingers nimbly typed on the computer keyboard. "Malcolm!" she exclaimed in surprise.

He whirled around, his features frozen momentarily in equal surprise. "Wha—what are you doing?" she asked, warning signals flashing brilliantly in her brain. They were warning signals she didn't—couldn't comprehend.

He grimaced and backed away from the computer. "Ah, Kelly, I'm afraid you've managed to get yourself into some trouble with your insistent snooping."

Kelly stared at him blankly. The warning signals silently screamed even louder in her head. *Silent Screams.* Kelly suddenly remembered the premise of the old script. "You..." she whispered as pieces of the puzzle began falling into place. The old script...the secret stairway...the strange malady that infected each of the men Malcolm had lived with. "*Silent Screams*... In the script a man drives his brother crazy." She stared at the old man in horror. "You drove Randolf crazy."

"Indeed." A small smile lifted one corner of his mouth. "That damned script. I knew if I allowed Randolf to take that part, he would once again rise to the top, once again be the successful man Daphne had married." He smiled broadly. "That script would have been Randolf's salvation, but it became mine instead. It's what gave me the tools to keep Randolf firmly under my power."

"And Gregory Mesker, and Dalton?" He looked so benign, so innocent. "But how? *Why?*" If what she thought was true, Kelly couldn't even begin to comprehend his evil. Again the alarms resounded in her head. She stumbled backward, turning to run back down the stairs, but Malcolm stopped her.

"I'm sorry, my dear. I can't let you go." He pulled a small handgun from his coat pocket, the barrel pointed at her.

Kelly's blood turned cold. She stared at Malcolm, unable to comprehend anything that was happening. "Why?" she repeated, needing to understand.

"I loved Daphne, loved her like I've never loved another woman. I should never have introduced her to Randolf. She became obsessed with him, possessed by him. Even when his career hit the skids her infatuation with him didn't waver. I figured the only way she would leave him was if she believed he was insane, and in order to make her believe that I had to make him insane." He smiled reflectively, the smile grotesque to Kelly. "It was child's play with Randolf. He was already so depressed about his career. All it took was drugs to alter his reality, whispers of Daphne betraying him. The stress of his lost career and the fear of losing her toppled him right into the pit of insanity."

"I . . . I don't understand. Was Daphne cheating on him?"

Malcolm laughed harshly, bitterly. "No. Daphne loved Randolf to distraction. She wouldn't look at another man . . . but the drugs made Randolf susceptible to my suggestions."

Kelly's head was spinning with questions... answers... and fear. "Where did you get the drugs?"

Malcolm shrugged. "My dear, drugs are an easy commodity when you have money. My chauffeur sees to my needs and is very well paid for his trouble... as was his father before him."

"So Randolf did kill Daphne?" she asked, wanting to keep the old man talking, waiting for his attention on her to waver, the aim of the gun's barrel to drift.

He stared at her, his eyes filled with a demented torment. He slowly shook his head. "I had it all figured out, except that. I didn't give Daphne's intelligence enough credit. She confronted me... that night immediately after the guests had left the party.... She suspected me of doing something to Randolf." His voice trembled, but the tremble didn't reach his hand. His grip was firm, the barrel of the gun glinting metallic in the overhead light.

"You killed her," Kelly replied softly.

"It was an accident," he said, his voice a tortured whine. "We argued at the top of the stairs.... She slipped and fell."

"So you shot her and then Randolf."

He looked at her helplessly. "There was nothing else to do. I'd have been ruined. I'd worked too hard to be a force in the industry. I couldn't let it all be destroyed. Gregory and Dalton had the same problem you have... a penchant for digging into the past. I warned you all to let it rest, leave it alone." He smiled charmingly, the quicksilver changing of expressions attesting to the extent of his madness. "I hope you understand my dear, this is nothing personal. It's merely self-preservation."

"What did you do to Dalton?" Kelly asked.

Malcolm shrugged. "Dalton was almost as easy as his grandfather. Drugs in his coffee, notes on his computer.... It didn't take long to shove him over the edge." He frowned for a moment. "Of course, I didn't expect him to start believing he was Randolf, but now it plays very well into my plans."

"Malcolm, you don't understand," Kelly protested. She knew there was more at work here than Malcolm's evil manipulations. Malcolm might think he was in control, but he wasn't. Randolf and Daphne were—and she had a feeling the ghosts weren't finished with their business yet. "Randolf really has come back from the dead. He really has possessed Dalton."

Malcolm laughed. "That's an amusing slant on things. But there's nothing supernatural at work here. *I'm* the only power in this house. And now it's time to end this all."

"End?" Kelly looked at him in horror.

"I wish there was another way. I've grown quite fond of you, but I'm afraid you're going to have to meet a tragic end." He motioned for her to leave the room, the gun barrel an effective escort out the doorway. "Just move nice and slowly down the stairs and to the landing."

"To the landing?" Kelly echoed faintly.

"Yes, you know, the landing at the top of the stairs where Daphne fell to her unfortunate death." As they walked slowly down the narrow stairway from Dalton's room, Kelly once again felt as if she was existing in a dream, a nightmare. Malcolm was responsible for Randolf and Daphne's deaths. He had been responsible for Gregory Mesker's death. She knew he wouldn't hesitate to kill again in order to save his reputation, cover his past crimes. She remembered that moment when she'd experienced Daphne's fall. Stark terror ripped through her. "They will talk about this for months to come," Malcolm said as they stepped onto the landing. "Stories will circulate, some people will speculate that the house is haunted. Imagine, the past tragedy repeating itself."

"You'll never get away with this," Kelly whispered, fear stealing her breath as she gripped the railing that led to the infamous staircase. She looked down the stairs, down to the spot on the floor where Daphne had died, all too able to imagine her own body lying there, crumpled and broken in death.

"Oh, but I will get away with it. I have before. Besides, all the people at the party tonight saw Dalton's madness. They'll all testify to the fact that he was insanely possessive with you. Nobody will be surprised that he pushed you down the stairs then shot himself."

"Daphne." Dalton's heart-wrenching cry came from downstairs.

Malcolm's eyebrows quirked upward. "If Dalton truly believes he's Randolf and you're Daphne, as angry as he sounds, I might not have to kill you after all.''

"What do you mean?" Kelly asked wildly.

"I'll let him kill you." Malcolm's smile widened, looking obscene and horrifyingly wicked. "He's angry with you, my dear. Very, very angry." He leaned over the railing. "Randolf. She's up here," he yelled down the stairs.

Kelly felt Dalton's approach before she saw him. The air vibrated with energy that expanded and crackled. He appeared at the foot of the stairs, his eyes bottomless pits of blackness as he stared up at her.

Kelly had been afraid of Malcolm, feared the gun he held in his hand, but the sight of Dalton slowly advancing up the stairs filled her with a horror that obscured everything else.

"Daphne," he whispered as he reached where she stood.

"She's cheating on you, Randolf," Malcolm said. "She's a whore who laughs at you behind your back."

"Yes," Dalton hissed, placing his hands on Kelly's shoulders. His eyes stared into hers, the pits of hell burning from them, consuming her in raging fires.

"She deserves to die, Randolf. Push her.... Let her fall. She deserves to die for betraying you." As Malcolm spoke, Dalton pulled Kelly closer to the edge of the stairs, his expression that of a man in a trance.

"No..." Kelly clung to the banister, fighting Dalton's strength as he moved her, inch by inch.

"It's the only way, Randolf, the only way you can be together forever. You have to push her. You must."

"Dalton...*no,*" Kelly screamed as together they teetered at the top of the stairs. The stairway yawned beneath them, dark and deadly. "I could never cheat on you. Dalton...I love you," she cried, tears choking her as she lost her grip on the banister and instead clung to him. "Dalton, I love you. *I love you,*" she repeated.

Dalton looked at her, the fires in his eyes abating. "Kelly?" His face twisted in confusion, looking first at her, then at Malcolm.

With an inhuman strength, he shoved Kelly away from the stairs, away from him. He dropped to one knee, his hands on either side of his head. "Help me," he roared, his voice steeped in torment and pain.

Static electricity snapped in the air and wind swirled around them, filling the air with the sweet scent of lilacs. Little pinpoints of light suddenly appeared, dancing, swirling, spinning themselves into a form...the distinctive form of a woman. She wore a long black dress, and each of her beautiful features was clear and visible.

"Daphne," Malcolm gasped. The gun clattered to the floor at his feet as he reached out to the ghost of the woman he'd loved. "Daphne...you've come back to me."

The woman smiled and floated down the stairs, beckoning Malcolm to follow her. He followed, a rapturous smile wreathing his face.

Kelly helped Dalton to his feet, and they hurried after the ghost as she led Malcolm down the stairs into the study and out the back door.

The night air was cold, the sky pitch-black with no stars, no moon to break the endless darkness. The deep night made the phantom Daphne glow with an unearthly brilliance, a beacon for Malcolm to follow.

He stumbled after her, hoarsely crying her name over and over again. He never hesitated, not even when she led him into the waves.

"Malcolm, wait," Kelly called, suddenly knowing the ghost's intent. But he was lost, lost to the haunting call of an obsessive love, the woman he had murdered.

Kelly was vaguely aware of Jeffrey running from the house, joining them as they watched the old man disappear into the ocean.

Minutes passed and nobody spoke. The energy was still in the air, flashes of lightning sparking the sky in the distance. Kelly held tight to Dalton. He seemed to be in a trance. She knew it wasn't over yet.

Suddenly Daphne came floating back across the water, a luminous figure of beauty. She hesitated where the waves broke onto the sandy shore. She raised her arms out to Dalton.

As if hypnotized by her, he moved forward.

"No," Kelly protested, grabbing hold of his arm, trying to hold him back from the lure of the ocean and Daphne. Had she gone through all of this madness only to lose Dalton to a phantom who enticed him toward the sea?

He struggled against her, his gaze fixed on the ghostly figure. Daphne's smile was soft, a lover's smile, and Dalton strained eagerly against Kelly's hold.

"Randolf, let him go," Kelly cried. "You don't need him anymore. Let him go!"

Dalton fell to his knees in the sand, and as he crumpled, a pale form arose from his inert body and the figure of Randolf materialized. Kelly stared, dumbstruck as the apparition of the dead movie star hovered for a moment, then sped to the water's edge, where he and his wife embraced.

The air around the pale ghostly couple snapped and sparked with blue arcs of electricity, and the dark clouds in the sky above them rolled and boiled. Kelly felt an enormous pressure in the air, the kind of pressure she'd always imagined would accompany a tornado.

As Randolf and Daphne kissed, their bodies shimmered with the light of a million fireflies. The pressure in the air increased and blue lightning flashed all around them. The two bodies became glowing orbs, and together, side by side, they shot off into the air, hanging momentarily like two stars in the sky, then disappearing over the horizon.

For a long moment the three on the beach said nothing, didn't move. The pressure that had been palpable in the air decreased and the wind that had whirled around them disappeared. Kelly felt tears stinging her eyes, knew that the two lovers were finally at peace, together once again, together for eternity.

"Awesome," Jeffrey finally said, breaking the spell of silence, of wonder.

"They're gone," Dalton said, rising slowly from the sand, reaching out to Kelly. She quickly moved to his side, supporting him as he stood staring out toward the water.

Above them the skies had cleared and a myriad of stars shone their brilliance down to the earth, painting them all in lush starlight. "But they're together for always... up there in the stars," Kelly replied softly. She shivered, awe filling her up inside. Dalton pulled her closer against the warmth of his body.

She looked back at the house. Her house. The interior lights radiated warmth and brightness out onto the surrounding sand. For the first time, Kelly sensed no shadows, no edges of darkness. The house called to her with loving whispers, and as she led Dalton toward it, she knew it would embrace them both with loving arms.

Kelly stood at the window, watching the dawn break over the water. The water patrol had left an hour earlier. They had found Malcolm's body and written up his death as an accidental drowning. Jeffrey had gone to his room for some much-needed sleep and Dalton had disappeared up to his study.

It was over. The madness was finally over. The spirits of Randolf and Daphne had been laid to rest. Kelly turned away from the window with a sigh. And now she had to figure out what was left behind, somehow sort out the residue of what was real and what had not been.

She loved Dalton. That was as crystal clear in her mind as the room surrounding her. But what did he feel for her? What had been Dalton's emotions and what had been Randolf's?

They had both been caught up in the obsession and passion of the past. Had any of that passion, any of the love Dalton had shown her, been real?

She heard footsteps descending the stairs and turned as Dalton entered the study, his arms laden with a large box of papers. "I've been housecleaning," he said, setting the box down next to the fireplace and picking up the poker.

"Housecleaning?" She watched curiously as he got a fire going, then sat down before it. He motioned for her to sit next to him.

"This is all my research for the book on Randolf and Daphne," he said, grabbing a handful of the papers and laying them on top of the flames.

"Dalton, what are you doing?" she asked incredulously as the papers caught fire, the intense blaze heating her face.

"I'm ridding myself of the baggage from the past." He watched the flames consume the papers, then turned to her and smiled. "I don't need to write the book anymore. The obsession is gone, the consuming fixation has disappeared. I know now that my grandfather was temperamental, obsessed with Daphne, possessively jealous, but he was *not* a murderer."

"That was what they wanted," Kelly said reflectively. "They wanted you to know the truth. They wanted to be vindicated."

"And I know I could write a thousand books offering up the truth of that night so long ago, but people will always believe what they want to believe." He fed more of the papers into the fire, staring for a long moment into the flames. "I don't need to tell the world, I just needed to know for myself. I'm free now from the past."

"I'm glad, Dalton," she said softly, studying his face in the fire's glow. It was a beautiful face now that the haunting shadows had dissipated. It was full of strength and character, . . . a face she loved.

He took her hand in his, his grasp warm and firm. "I'll always be grateful to you, Kelly. It would have been easy for you to run from me in fear, leave me to Randolf and Malcolm."

This time it was Kelly who stared into the fire, remembering the moments when she had experienced vicariously Daphne's final fall down the stairs, those moments when she and Dalton had made love and she'd lost herself in the mists of the past. "I think there were times when I was just a little possessed myself, when Daphne worked through me."

She thought again of Dalton's words. Gratitude. He'd always be grateful to her. Apparently the love radiating from him, the deep emotional bond she'd felt, had been borrowed from Randolf and had been directed at Daphne.

Sorrow welled up inside her, burning her eyes with unshed tears. She removed her hand from his and stood up, not wanting to feel his spirit, the soul she knew she'd love forever.

Throughout the hours of the night, while the water patrol had searched for Malcolm, Kelly had thought about the vibrations she'd always picked up from people. She'd realized that she'd never been able to feel anything from Jeffrey because he was a teenager, floundering in a search for self-identity. She'd also realized that the reason she hadn't been able to feel anything from Malcolm was because his soul was so black...too black for her to comprehend. But Dalton's... She cleared her throat, swallowing the threat of tears. "So, now that you aren't going to write your book, I guess you'll be going back to the city."

He threw a few more sheets of paper on the fire, then stood up and faced her. "Actually, I have another story in mind for a book, a fictional fantasy about possession."

Kelly forced a smile. "Sounds pretty incredible to me."

"Perhaps, but I'd like to stay here and work on it if it's all right with you."

"Of course it's all right with me," she replied. Oh, how was she going to see him every day, remember the passion that had flamed so hot between them, and now settle for a landlord/tenant relationship?

"Of course, before I decide to stay here, we really need to discuss my room arrangements."

She looked at him blankly. "Your room arrangements?"

He nodded, standing so close to her she could smell his familiar scent—not bay rum, but the scent of Dalton. "My room is terribly drafty... and lonely. I'd be much happier with a roommate."

"A roommate?" she echoed.

His dark eyes flared with fire. "Kelly, I love you." He reached out and drew her into his embrace.

A sob escaped her as she felt him surrounding her, warming her. "Oh, Dalton, I love you, too. But I was so afraid... afraid that none of it was real, that it was all Randolf and his possession—"

He interrupted her with a kiss, a kiss of such suppressed passion, such tender love, that Kelly felt her heart expand. He broke the kiss, his gaze looking deep into her eyes. "Kelly, my love for you was the only thing real through all of this. It pulled me through, it made me fight against the drugs, the madness of Malcolm's manipulations. I love you, Kelly, and it's as strong as the love that existed between Randolf and Daphne. It will last throughout eternity."

Kelly smiled up at him, tears of happiness shimmering in her eyes. "Then I guess you've got yourself a roommate."

"There's one other thing we need to do," he said. "We need to get some carpenters in here to take out all the hidden stairs and passageways. I don't want anyone to be able to use them ever again for evil purposes."

"I agree," Kelly replied, "and I intend to keep you in my bed and at my side throughout every night, so you'll never have to come through any secret passageway to find me. All you'll need to do is look beside you and I'll be there."

The fires in Dalton's eyes exploded, and with a soft groan he once again covered her lips with his. Kelly surrendered to the brilliance of his passion as it reached out for hers. She yielded to the flames his touch always evoked. She felt his soul reaching out to her, and she welcomed it, allowing it to possess hers, knowing this would prove the sweetest possession she'd ever known.

Around them, the house sighed in melodious contentment.

* * * * *

SPRING
fancy
'94

**They're sexy, single...
and about to get snagged!**

Passion is in full bloom as love catches
the fancy of three brash bachelors. You won't
want to miss these stories by three of
Silhouette's hottest authors:

CAIT LONDON
DIXIE BROWNING
PEPPER ADAMS

Spring fever is in the air this March—
and there's no avoiding it!

Only from

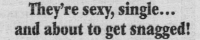 *Silhouette*®

where passion lives.

1

FREE
BOOK COUPON

TO RECEIVE YOUR COPY OF THE *SILHOUETTE SHADOWS COLLECTION* RETURN SIX (6) FREE BOOK COUPONS PLUS CHECK OR MONEY ORDER FOR $1.50 FOR DELIVERY IN THE SPECIAL REPLY ENVELOPE PROVIDED. PLEASE DO NOT SEND CASH.

SHDBP-3A

1

FREE
BOOK COUPON

TO RECEIVE YOUR COPY OF THE *SILHOUETTE SHADOWS COLLECTION* RETURN SIX (6) FREE BOOK COUPONS PLUS CHECK OR MONEY ORDER FOR $1.50 FOR DELIVERY IN THE SPECIAL REPLY ENVELOPE PROVIDED. PLEASE DO NOT SEND CASH.

IT'S YOURS
FREE!

SILHOUETTE SHADOWS COLLECTION

FREE BOOK COUPON

As a member of Silhouette's newest line, you are eligible for a special gift. Save this free book coupon. Six coupons entitle you to receive a free copy of the *Silhouette Shadows Collection*, three chilling novels of danger and romance.

ACCT. #

YOUR NAME

ADDRESS

CITY   STATE/PROV.   ZIP/POSTAL CODE

090KBC

SAVE THIS COUPON

IT'S YOURS
FREE!

IT'S YOURS
FREE!

SILHOUETTE SHADOWS COLLECTION

FREE BOOK COUPON

As a member of Silhouette's newest line, you are eligible for a special gift. Save this free book coupon. Six coupons entitle you to receive a free copy of the *Silhouette Shadows Collection*, three chilling novels of danger and romance.

ACCT. #

YOUR NAME

ADDRESS

CITY   STATE/PROV.   ZIP/POSTAL CODE

090KBC

SAVE THIS COUPON

IT'S YOURS
FREE!